The Varieties of Jewish Experience

TINY STORIES, LITTLE STORIES, SHORT STORIES,
AND EVEN A NOVELLA!

LARRY LEFKOWITZ

Fomite
Burlington, VT

ISBN-13: 978-1-959984-05-4
Library of Congress Control Number: requested

Fomite
58 Peru Street
Burlington, VT 05401
www.fomitepress.com
02-22-2023

for
my wife
my children
my grandchildren

Contents

The Lady in the Bay

At he time of the call, which was dutifully recorded as having come at six o'clock in the morning to the Jaffa district police station, a record-breaking hamsin hung over the city. When Sergeant Dihon listlessly picked up the phone, an agitated voice on the other end of the line reported: "There's a woman out there in the bay chained to a rock with her liver exposed and a bird is gnawing on it!"

A silence ensued at the police end of the line, partly induced by the natural nonchalance of Sergeant Dihon — who is, after all, a veteran in the Jaffa District and one who has "seen everything", as he himself is prone to saying — and partly induced by the fact that the good sergeant has suffered over the years not a few cuckoo people ringing him up.

Nor can the influence of the hamsin be discounted. A hamsin unfailingly raises the level of eccentricity. Dihon was already dabbing at his brow with a handkerchief, despite the early hour. The caller's report contained so many novel elements that Dihon was tempted to advise him to "Say shecheanu and hang up the phone. But remembering the injunction against being happy at the misfortunes of another, he asked finally, "Her liver, eh?"

"Right."

"Chained to a rock."

"The woman, yes."

Dihon returned the handkerchief to his pocket. "It's probably a publicity stunt — or a political protest — some leftist chaining herself to a rock. Except for the liver part. You're sure she wasn't holding a giant pizza which attracted some kind of bird?"

"I'm sure. I know a liver when I see one."

"By this I take it that you mean that her liver is drooping, or whatever livers do when they are outside of the body.

"It's drooping."

"And what is gnaw—" Dihon stopped, unable to bring himself to repeat the daffy sentence.

The caller saved him the trouble. "A bird is gnawing at it."

"Oh well, that explains it," said Sergeant Dihon affably. "I mean, if the liver is there, why won't a bird make the best of it? Your ordinary Jaffa bird isn't very discerning."

"You don't believe me," said the voice on the other end of the line in an offended tone.

"Well, let us say there are elements in your story that raise some questions."

"Listen, commandant —"

"Sergeant."

"Sergeant — I'm simply doing my duty as a citizen. Women-liver-bird — those are the facts. What you do with those facts is up to you."

"Ok, ok, faithful citizen, we'll check it out."

The caller replied in a mollified tone, "Please do so, I'm sure she'll appreciate it."

The moment he hung up the phone, the Sergeant forgot about the woman and the bird.

But not for long. A second caller reported a woman chained to a rock and a bird pecking at her liver. "You sure it's not her intestines?" Dihon asked, slamming down the phone.

When a third and then a fourth call reported a similar story, Dihon's assessment that a group of his wife's family members were having their little joke began to dissipate. Twenty calls later, he summoned Weinstein, the newest policeman in the station, into his office. He had taken Weinstein under his wing, and now it was Weinstein's turn to pay him back.

"Listen, Weinstein, I've been the recipient of a gift box in the form of some calls complaining about some woman in the bay whose — well, you take the launch and see if anything unusual is happening to someone chained to a rock."

"Chained to a rock?"

"Yeah, that's what the callers said. Probably a publicity stunt for a new perfume." Dihon didn't mention the liver.

Half a hundred calls later — which calls caused

Dihon increasingly to rub lightly the hand-shaped charm which he kept on a chain in his pocket to guard against the evil eye in the hope that it would work against the cursed deluge of calls — was back. There would have been far more calls, but Dihon, tiring of repeating like a man in a trance that the matter "was under investigation," had taken the phone off the hook. It was against regulations, but Dihon, as befitted one experienced with the years, was notably flexible when it came to regulations.

Weinstein, a type usually anchored in reality, stood in front of him, white-faced, and in a kind of stupor — both of which Dihon attributed to the hamsin. In contrst to the immobility of his body, Weinstein's hands fluttered in the air like birds scattered by a sudden noise, while their owner stood incapable of saying anything for some moments. "Sergeant Dihon," he finally managed to stammer, "There's a lady chained to a rock out in the bay and…" he paused.

"And a bird is chewing on her liver," Dihon said evenly.

Weinstein's jaw dropped. "How did you know?"

Dihon pounced on the helpless rookie, slamming his fist on the desk. "Who put you up to this, Weinstein?"

"Nobody, sir. I saw it with my own eyes. That bird, like something out of a Poe novel. And that liver drooping like something in a Salvadore Dali painting. I'll never eat liver again. Not even my mother's chopped liver. Especially not chopped liver."

"Come with me, Weinstein."

"Where?"

Dihon gave him one of those penetrating looks that had put many a criminal on the defensive. "Where else? To the cursed woman on the cursed rock with the cursed liver."

Dihon put Levy in charge of things while he was gone, giving him a list of things to do. And one not to do — which Dihon emphasized: not to put the phone back on the hook.

When Sergeant Dihon returned, in a stupor not unlike that of Weinstein when he had returrned, officer Levy informed him that Zubulun the mayor wished to see him. At once. It didn't require an interpretation by Rashi to know why.

Although relations in the past between Dihon and Zubulun the mayor had been, in the main, leisurely and calm, on this occasion the mayor, after a mumbled greeting to Dihon, hurried him into a seat in the mayor's office and hovered over the policeman like some nervous bird of prey. "What's your opinion on how we should handle this… problem in the bay, Sergeant?"

Dihon didn't bat an eye. 'I'm not sure we can arrest her for exposing her liver in public. Other parts of the body, yes, but…"

"I don't want you to arrest her. There are certain problems with that approach."

Dihon replied that he would be happy to carry out any approach of the mayor's once the mayor would reveal it.

The mayor walked around in a circle for some

minutes. From time to time, he looked at Dihon as if he wanted to say something, but each time he seemed to decide against it. Then His Honor stopped and glanced at the policeman. "I remembered something from my studies at the university. Something about a Greek myth about a woman — called Andromeda — being chained to a rock and a bird nibbling at her entrails."

"Really?" Dihon said neutrally.

"I rung up Professor Bromfman at Tel Aviv University — he's an expert on mythology. He confirmed the accuracy of my memory."

"About the Greek myth of this Andrea and the hungry bird."

"Andromeda. Yes. The facts fit the myth exactly."

Dihon thought that "facts" didn't go with "myth", but it wasn't for a sergeant to give the mayor a lesson in definitions.

"Well, maybe we can treat her as a myth and ignore her."

"Good try, Dihon. There are, however, complications."

"Such as?"

"Our relations with the Greek Government are presently at a sensitive period. Now is not the time to challenge one of their myths if we can avoid it. In addition, our Minister of Tourism is on my back. He sees a huge tourist potential for sightseeing via a fleet of mini-boats. Notwithstanding that the harbor authorities already consider her a traffic hazard because of all the boat people gawking at her."

"And the Minister of Health probably has an opinion on the matter — I am refering to the exposed liver."

But the mayor wasn't listening.

"That bird — maybe the zoo people can capture him. That would help the liver aspect. And then maybe a team of surgeons from Belinson can stuff it back in."

Dihon shook his head. "Your solutions are too practical. You're dealing with a myth. You Ashkenazis think that reason can solve everything. Believe me, you've got something a lot stickier here. You might do better trying 'The Radiance of Jaffa.'"

"'The Radiance of Jaffa.'?"

"The wonder rabbi. My wife's family swears by him. Her brother — "

Dihon stopped. The last thing he needed was to bring his wife's brother into this.

After Dihon had left, the mayor decided that maybe the policeman was right. In any event, it was incumbunt on him to try. The mayor arranged for his publicity director's cousin who he knew was a disciple of the Radiance to approach him about the problem.

"Well?" said the mayor to the cousin of the publicity director when the latter brought the former to the mayor to report about his meeting with The Radiance.

"The Radiance was very interested in your problem. He wondered if perhaps the bird wasn't Ziz-Shaddi, the bird Hashem created on the fifth day of creation. The bird that the righteous, at the End of Days, will gather to feast upon at the messianic banquet at which the heavenly waiter will be Moses himself! But, the Radiance added, that on the fifth day, the same day that Hashem created the birds, He created the fishes."

Zubulun the mayor interrupted him. "What do the fishes have to do with the matter? We only have a bird!"

The cousin spread his hands wide, not unlike the Radiance himself. "Both birds and fishes swim, birds in the air and fishes in the water. So the Radiance said. And Leviathan was created with the fishes. Just as Ziz-Shaddi is King of the birds, so Leviathan is King of the sea."

Once again, the mayor stopped him. "We have a big enough problem without your bringing Leviathan into this."

"I didn't. The Radiance did. There is a connection, as The Radiance pointed out. Ziz rests its feet on the fins of Leviathan. In the End of Days, Leviathan will be torn by Ziz, and the latter slaughtered by Moses. Both Leviathan and Ziz will be served at the banquet of the righteous."

"Very nice," said the mayor. That's it? — that's all The Radiance had to say about our problem?"

For some moments the cousin did not speak. When he did, he said: "And then there is the raven."

"Aha," said the mayor, rubbing his hands. "Our bird."

Needless to say, the country was soon agog with the matter. And soon the world, too, was captured by the "Lady in the Bay," a she had come to be called by CNN, and "Andromeda" by Sky News. And just when it looked like the UN Secretary General was going to come to personally investigate the matter (despite Israel's protest), one morning she was gone. And so were the chain, the liver, and the bird.

Nobody could explain why. Some thought that maybe it was because Jaffa Bay was polluted. Some because the hamsin had ended. Other reasons were given, especially in the Knesset, most of them of a partisan political nature that do not bear repeating here.

Later there were reportings of a similar sighting of a woman chained to a rock near Alcatraz Island in San Francisco Bay, with the bird performing similarly on her similarly distended liver. And another sighting near the Statue of Liberty.

"That's it," opined Dihon to Weinstein. "Andromeda got a big head on her and went to America."

"It's logical," agreed Weinstein. "There are a couple of liver specialists there with a wide-world reputation."

"That could explain it," agreed Dihon. "Those cheapskates on Mt. Olympus probably calculated initially that they could get it done faster and cheaper closer to home."

The new revisionist historians will claim it all never happened. But they are the last people to depend on when it comes to the subject of myths.

The Golem of Jerusalem

The idea came to Shmulik in a dream, perhaps induced by an over-ingestion of *kubeh* soup for dinner. On a wider subconscious level, Shmulik's life during the present football season prepared him for the dream. Because day and night one thought ate at him: how to save Betar Jerusalem from the ignominy of descending from the premier league to the second league. In his dream he created a Golem that would rescue Betar.

At first, he told no one about his dream. Then he told his two best friends, fanatical supporters of Betar, of course (otherwise they would not be his closest friends) about his plan.

"To build a Golem?" Yuval said.

"Are you normal?" was Avi's response.

"Why not? There are precedents."

"Isn't it a bit — dangerous?" Yuval said.

"Dangerous? There are terrorist attacks left and right and you talk about being dangerous."

"Still…"

"Look, my cousin is into Kabbalah. He is a staunch Betar fan. He has already agreed to help us."

Avi raised an eyebrow. "Us?"

Shmulik answered him in a tone of annoyance. "Of course, us. First of all, my cousin will need help to create a Golem. He says that one person alone cannot create a Golem, that it is written: 'Two are better than one.' And if two are better than one, three are better than two, and four… well, you get his point. And besides, true fans of Betar would do *anything* to help the team."

Yuval rubbed his chin doubtfully. "Perhaps we should go to Rabbi Kaduri. He's an expert in Kabbalah. Let *him* build the Golem."

"No, no," replied Shmulik. "This has to remain a secret. Just the four of us."

Avi nodded, "Like the four musketeers. 'All for one and one for all.'"

"'All for the Golem and the Golem for Betar!'" cried Yuval.

Shmulik raised a calming hand. "My cousin said that the first step is to go to the Kidron stream to get some mud."

"Mud?" exclaimed Yuval.

"To build the Golem, golem."

"Why not," asked Avi, "go to Teddy Kolik Stadium, Betar is stuck in the mud there."

"Be respectful," Shmulik cautioned him.

"One thing's sure," Yuval said. "Betar needs help and fast."

"Right," agreed Shmulik. "One game Kubika is good, another game he disappears. One game Telkar shows he knows how to play, another game you wonder if he isn't the groundskeeper. The team's defense is ok, but they don't score goals. The coach has tried more combinations of players than the prime minister has with his ministers. Nothing seems to work. Until he finds the suitable players and the suitable system, Betar will be in the second league. *That's* why we need a Golem. A Golem that will be the super player which will make all systems superfluous and will keep Betar in the premier league."

Yuval scratched his head. "Ok, we're agreed. Betar needs a Golem-player. And we'll build him there — at the Kidron?"

"Yes," said Shmulik. My cousin said that Rabbi Loew of Prague took three men with him to get mud from the bank of the Moldau, and built a Golem. We'll do the same at the Kidron. At night. Don't worry, if he looks a bit strange, we'll bring him back in the trunk of the car. But I hope he'll look like a regular Betar player and can sit in back with you two."

"Who sits in front with you?"

"My cousin. He's a kabbalist. He deserves the honor. Besides, it may take two guys to hold the Golem. He might be a bit frisky at first."

Yuval paled at this. Avi, stronger in build, made a muscle to show he was ready

And so it came about that a week later the quartet of devoted Betar fans armed with shovels drove to the banks of the Kidron to dig its muddy clay, just as Rabbi Loew of Prague and his helpers dug the clay from the banks of the Moldau. The same river which gave its name to the musical composition 'The Moldau' which provided the melody upon which the Israeli national anthem 'Hatikvah' was based. When Shmulik informed the others of this fact, Yuval and Avi took it as a positive omen. Nevertheless, they appeared doubtful, and even Shmulik looked less confident. The cousin sought to reassure them. "It's been done many times before. In the third century, Rabbi Rava created a Golem. True, Rabbi Hanina and Rabbi Oshaya were less successful, managing to produce only a very small calf, which they ate. Rabbi Shlomo ben Gabirol was more successful, he created a woman Golem. Ben Sira and his father created a Golem. Rabbi Aharon of Baghdad and Rabbi Hananel produced Golems. So did Rabbi Elazar of Worms, and also Abraham Abulafia. Rabbi Loew created his Golem according to the book of Yezirah. So you see," the cousin assured them, "there's 'nothing new under the sun.'" This history seemed to instill a measure of confidence in the others. Did they succeed? Is it not said "Four went out and five came back"? But let us not get ahead of our story.

We return to the bank of the Kidron and that fateful night. According to the cousin's instructions, his three pupils began digging. When he signaled that they had dug enough clay, they stopped. From his pocket the cousin removed a butter knife, and began creating a clay imitation the size of a man, a large solid man with the strong molded calves of the super-player.

"Try to make him look like Betar's most famous player, Malmillian," Avi urged.

"What's wrong with Ochana?" asked Yuval

"It doesn't matter what he looks like, Shmulik replied, "so long as he looks impressive, and, more importantly, unstoppable."

The cousin stooped and molded the form's face, at times using the butter knife, and then, full of energy, proceeded to put the finish on the rest of him, and then started to pray, rocking back and forth.

To the amazement of the other three, the clay began to smoke and to heat dull red and then a brighter red (which oddly discomfited Avi, since it reminded him of the color of Betar's rival, Hapoel Tel Aviv), then, cooling, turned an orange color, and then dulled almost to skin color. It was no longer clay but flesh at which they stared. The man then sprouted hair and a nose, eyes, lips.

Now the cousin turns to Shmulik and tells him what he has to say and repeat, and instructs him to circle the body seven times.

The chest of the Golem starts to heave slowly. His lips part. A breath that is a deep long groan issues from him (some will contend later that it was more like a cheer), and the man of clay begins to stir. The eyes open, at first unseeing, then he looks and sees them. He is alive, and with him the hopes of Betar.

The Golem stares at the cousin. "Master," he says.
"Betar, Betar is your master," the cousin corrects him.
"Betar," the Golem repeats.

For two months Smulik kept the Golem hidden in his house (a divorcee, he lived alone — most of the time). During this period, he educated the Golem on the rudiments of living in Jerusalem in the beginning of the third millennium. This included teaching him Hebrew. The Golem turned out to be a surprisingly quick learner (this may have had something to do with the Hebrew letters by which he was created) and by the end of two months had just about reached high-school level. That will do for his purposes, or rather our purposes, mused Shmulik. The potential player was ready to be turned over to Betar for training.

Shmuli, with Yuval and Avi present for support, transported the Golem over to where Betar practiced. There they introduced him to the coach. "This is, ah, Moti. Moti… Goldman," Shmulik said. "We are convinced that he can help Betar."

The coach looked him over briefly. "Well, if the way he is built is any indication, he could indeed be a big help to us. Our attack is weak. We need somebody who can put the ball in the opponent's goal — and we need him fast."

"He's a bit… rough," said Shmulik. "But you're the one to turn him into a good player. A great player, even. A second Mamillian. Oh, one other thing, he needs a place to stay." Shmullik was tired of housing him. It was like living together with a giant St. Bernard under his roof.

"He can room with our new Brazilian player. He complains he feels lonely."

"It's hard to feel lonely with the Go — with Goldman around," Shmulik attested.

A week later Shmulik got a call from the coach. "You'd better come down to practice tomorrow, I need to talk to you."

Shmulik tried to fathom from the coach's tone whether he was pleased or displeased, yet something in that "you'd better" nagged at him.

The first thing that Shmulik noticed when he arrived at the practice field was that the Golem was sitting on the bench, hunched over, kind of looking like the famous sculpture 'The Thinker.'

"How's he doing?" Shmulik asked the coach.

"He's big and strong and runs with the force of a bulldozer."

"Sounds encouraging," Shmulik grinned, pleased.

"Except for one thing," the coach answered.

Shmulik's grin faded. "And what's that?"

"He can't keep the ball on the field. He kicks it and the ball soars way above the goal — and I mean way above. He's simply too powerful. Never saw anything like it. A couple of times when he kicked the ball, it exploded from the force of his kick."

"Can't you get him to kick softer?"

"Goldman doesn't know from soft. 'Soft' isn't in his vocabulary, which, by the way, is somewhat limited."

"I thought it was sufficient… I mean, you don't need him to pass the college entrance exams. You need him to score goals."

"He's simply too powerful. He's like the Golem of Prague."

"Yeah, there is a similarity," admitted Shmulik.

"And there's another thing. Half my players are wounded from him. He runs down the field — not dribbling the ball, he can't since once he touches it with his foot, it's gone — and — CRACK — anyone guarding him is run over. He doesn't seem to grasp what a yellow card is, let alone a red card. You can have him back, he's no help to us. But *you* tell him. I don't want any physical resistance. The guy seems to get a little bigger each day. And I have to tell you, there's some kind of crazy rumor going around the city, apparently it started in kabbalistic circles, that he's a Golem — the kind from Prague, not the occasional golem I've had on the team. There's even a rumor that Hapoel Tel Aviv has approached Rabbi Lau about creating a Golem for them. Golem or not, he's yours. Thanks, but no thanks. Oh, and our Brazilian player slipped out of the country. I should have known something wasn't right since the week before he went around repeating the word "voodoo" and crossing himself all the time. Before his last practice, he insisted on sacrificing a chicken prior to entering the playing field, a custom I had thought limited to a few of our more esoteric fans."

Shmulik took the Golem home, after only with

difficulty succeeding to get him into his car. He immediately invited Avi and Yuval over to tell them the bad news.

"After all our effort," said Yuval.

"Yeah," sighed Avi, too crushed by the news to say any more.

"What do we do now?" asked Yuval.

"I think the first thing to do is to call my cousin over. I suspect that he has done a little boasting to his kabbalistic cronies."

A half-hour later the cousin arrived. "We'll have to destroy him," he decided after Shmulik brought him up to date.

Avi was shocked. "Destroy him? I've kind of gotten used to him."

"Yeah, he grows on you," agreed Yuval.

"I feared all along it might come to this," the cousin opined. "The history of Golem creation is not without its share of failures. But I hoped he could help Betar win the championship first, or at least help it remain in the premier league. Still, it had to end sometime. After all, he grows a bit each day, Golems do that. If he had been created for a basketball team, he would be able to play a couple of seasons, maybe even three or four, before he got too big."

"Maybe the Hapoel Jerusalem basketball team could use him," Avi proposed. "Usually I don't like to help a Hapoel team, but there isn't a Betar basketball team here anymore, and at least it would be for a Jerusalem team."

Shmulik shook his head in dismissal. "No, every time he put in a dunk shot, the basket would be ripped off the backboard and put a dent in the floor. Let's face it, we made a mistake. We'll have to bring him to the Kidron and carry out the reverse ceremony in order to restore him to dust and return him to the mud of the Kidron.

And so it was that the Golem of Jerusalem, as he came to be called, became a legend. There are those who will swear on their mother's name that the last word he emitted was "Betar." This, too, has become a part of the legend. At least among Betar fans.

Oh Bartalina!

He looked up and saw the photograph of the luscious figure and sensual face of Bartalina Shloshberg, the supermodel, in a giant reproduction that took up most of the front of a tall building. A 25 times life-size version of his mental beloved. A portrait that was repeated throughout the city on other tall buildings in what was billed as "the greatest advertising campaign this city has ever seen."

How fortunate he was that the current advertising mantra was to use the images of beautiful women to advertise everything from cars to furniture, from restaurants to paint. In this case, Bartalina Shloshberg's line of cosmetics, line of fashion, line of perfume, line of underwear. Each photograph of her emphasized a particular product she was marketing. In his eyes, there was no woman more beautiful than Bartalina Shloshberg. A loner, never successful with meeting women, he fantasized all kinds of fantasies with Bar. Even before the current advertising campaign put her tantalizing self everywhere he went, he would spend hours gazing at her, his Bar, in magazines and on television.

He was sorry he could not mount a scaffold and get close enough to plant a kiss on her beauteous lips, as he used to plant on her face in the fashion magazines. Her pictures lined the walls of his bedroom. And now looking up at her magnificent, titanic presence, he feasted on her large luminescent eyes, lips like the curve of the sea, her nose straight and smooth as an ivory tower, breasts like twin Catskill Mountains that sloped down to a belly flat as the beach at the Jersey shore. To climb to her, to touch her breasts exposed above her pupik-revealing body-shirt like two halves of a giant honeydew melon, to move his hands across her smooth legs like those of a female Colossus revealed by her mini. An offer of the ultimate in tactile pleasure.

A voracious reader, he was mindful of Gulliver's meeting with the giant women, the Brobdingnagians, who boasted giant breasts, six feet tall, the nipples half as large as his head. He envied Gulliver, who lay "at full length in their bosoms." He repressed the thought, in connection to Bar's wonderful features, that he, like Gulliver, could easily fit into the pock marks of the giant women's faces. And then he was cheered by the realization that Bar's very own cosmetic line could alleviate this negative feature, though any cream would surely pose a problem as it would be larger than his body and a threat to his breathing.

Did he imagine it, or was a musk-like perfume wafted electronically or mechanically from the pictures of Bartalina Shloshberg? Surely, one of Bar's line of perfumes. He liked to use her perfumes instead of male aftershave. Particularly when he wanted to engage in lengthy fantasizing, particularly when he couldn't sleep at night. And to induce sleep, he counted Bartalina Shloshbergs jumping over him, and occasionally falling on him.

He would spend nights roaming the city, from one picture of Bartalina Shloshberg to another, and then another. Desire stimulated on one hand but, alas, at three in the morning, he was painfully aware of feeling very small, his life solitary and lonely, and that he would never reach Bartalina Shloshberg. Like a man in a daze or trance, he found himself climbing a ladder, to touch his beloved. To kiss her enticing feet, and then to work his way upward.

Alas, in his zeal, he lost his footing and fell.

In the hospital, he was hugged by Bartalina Shloshberg herself! Hearing about his plight, she came to visit him, accompanied by her personal photographer and her personal cosmetician. The famous picture of Bartalina Shloshberg hugging him appeared on the cover of Vogue.

Afterwards, in life, he never married. No woman of flesh and blood could meet the challenge posed by the towering face and figure of Bartalina Shloshberg. Not even Bartalina Shloshberg herself.

A Minyan of Two

Lord of mercy, guide your servant according to your will, intoned Rivlin. The first sun of the double star had almost set. Sabbath had come. Rivlin had set his calendar to the nearer of the two stars, according to the rabbis' ruling in such cases. And what did the rabbis suggest if you were not only the only Jew on a planet, but also the only person? For a short time, admittedly; his partner was due back soon after a minor operation on the nearest medical planet. This was a violation of the galaxy regulation prohibiting an individual serving alone on a planet, but budgetary limitations had ruled out a strict compliance with the regulation since his partner was scheduled to return in a few days.

Spread above me your tent of peace. After he had finished the opening prayer, Rivlin paused to look at his two dwindling shadows, made by the first barely visible star, before singing: *Go, my beloved toward the queen, the face of Sabbath we will receive.* He stopped. The line was correct.

Only he hadn't sung it. Or had he? Had the mind-losing process begun? It was the very thing that the regulation prohibiting less than two partners to serve on a planet had meant to avoid.

The planet was devoid of vegetation; its sole justification for their dual — now single — presence was the magnetic mining potential a man-less probe had detected. A team would arrive soon to prepare mining operations. He and his partner were there to prepare for their arrival.

Rivlin poked at the sandy surface with his boot. A small whirlwind rose and then collapsed. He thought of the prophet Ezekiel. He felt an overwhelming need to continue with the Sabbath service. *And a city will be built,* he sang, but the prayer had not helped. How could it? It had not come from him. It seemed to come from somewhere outside of him, from somewhere to his left. From behind a small hill. Despite his fear, Rivlin began to run in its direction. The song increased in intensity. Rivlin rounded the hill as the last line was sung: *We will receive.*

A small creature, approximately a meter in height, stood facing in the direction — of Earth! The creature gave a slight bow. Rivlin stood aghast. He recited the blessing upon seeing an unusual person. He had the uncanny feeling that the creature was reciting the same blessing about him.

"What are you?" Rivlin wanted to shout. "Who are you?" he heard himself ask in a quieter voice. He noticed that the creature wore a skullcap.

"Chaim," the creature said in a friendly voice.

Rivlin stood mute. Dumbfounded.

"What did you expect, the Golem of Prague?" the creature asked.

Rivlin felt like weeping. And escaping. The creature seemed to anticipate him. "It's forbidden to go outside the measured area allowed for the Sabbath," it said. "You didn't take this into consideration. It was understandable considering the circumstances. But now that the matter is cleared up for you…"

Rivlin didn't know whether to laugh or cry. "Are you Jewish?"

"Nu, what else? You heard me praying. A shayner yid," it said.

Rivlin would have held on to a tree if the planet had had trees. Unfortunately, nothing vertical existed on it, except hills and a hill couldn't be grasped by a man — even one who had gone over the edge. Here, on a minor uninhabited planet six hundred and twelve light years from where Moses had seen a burning bush, there were no bushes. And yet there was Chaim.

"You don't look Jewish," Rivlin couldn't stop himself from saying. And why stop himself — the creature could apparently read his thoughts.

A high-pitched chuckle rippled out from the throat of the creature. It shook its head. "I suppose not, from your viewpoint. Let me assure you that I am very Jewish. Where I come from, I'm one of the first for a minyan. Besides, I have a Jewish mother."

"But what are you doing here?" Rivlin asked, looking around involuntarily at the sand increasingly darkening as the second sun sunk below the horizon.

The creature winked, or seemed to. The construction of its three eyes made it difficult to be sure. They had shut and opened together in about twice the time that an earth human's eyes would have required to carry out the same operation. "Shabbos was coming. A Jew shouldn't pray alone. I would have liked to bring eight others to form a minyan but they only sent me..." The creature's stubby appendages fluttered in explanation. "Budgetary constraints," he added.

"You were sent?!"

"The rabbinate. They know you are Orthodox. They also know I am Orthodox. Incidentally, our planet is Orthodox — except for a smaller Conservative congregation, and an even smaller Reform. My planet is the closest planet that has a substantial Jewish population. The rabbinate didn't want you to be alone on the Sabbath."

Rivlin wanted to embrace Chaim.

Chaim sensed it. "Feel free," he said. "You Earth residents are less emotional compared to us. Even the Jewish ones."

But not Rivlin at that moment, who was deeply moved because they had sent him someone for the Sabbath.

"How can I thank you," he said.

"No need," Chaim replied. "Absolutely no need." To cover his own emotions, Chaim began to recite the evening prayer, and when he reached and arranges the stars in the heavens, Rivlin joined him. The only sound heard on the planet, it reached to its every corner and beyond.

Play it Again, Woody

Silverberg begged off the football victory party. "Count me out guys, I have to visit a sick aunt."

"You're kidding," his fraternity brothers chided him. "The best tackle in the whole damned state, maybe the whole country — a sick aunt? Rapport smacked him on the back. I'll bet you got a hot number lined up."

The aunt story was indeed a fabrication. Silverberg did have a rendezvous which he wanted to keep secret — at the local art film cinema. 'Play it Again, Sam' was playing (again). Silverberg loved the movie, had seen it countless times. The only part of the film he didn't like was when 'Bogie' was giving Woody advice on how to score with girls. For Silverberg, as for the rest of the Woody buffs, the protagonist of the film was really Woody. Woody was not only the hero of the film for Silverberg, but the image with whom he identified. He, too, had a problem with girls.

Nobody knew it. Silverberg covered it as best he could. The girls swarmed around him like — like girls around a football hero. They talked football and wanted to hear football, so football was what they got. Silverberg would rather talk about art or music or cinema. But whenever he tried, they guffawed. They thought he was putting them on. He no longer tried not to put them on.

One time he found himself sitting on a campus bench next to a lit major; he could tell she was a lit major by the titles of the books she had stacked next to her on the bench. One was Ulysses. Ulysses!" he exclaimed, unable to contain his enthusiasm. "A great book." She took one look at him — and one look was all that was required — everybody knew him — and nearly fell off the bench from laughing. Finnegans Wake, he threw at her frantically. She was now holding her stomach, tears running down her cheeks. Silverberg would have loved to ask her to see 'Play it Again, Sam', but she might have been seized by convulsions from laughing.

And so, Silverberg found himself once again, alone, with Sam, with Woody. The film opened with the famous final scene from 'Casablanca'. Woody is watching it in a movie theater — alone. The scene shifts to where Woody's wife leaves him. At least I'm not unhappily married, Silverberg consoled himself. It seemed to him that Woody looked look directly at him from the screen as if he had actually heard him.

I empathize so completely with Woody that I feel as if he is paying attention to me, thought Silverberg.

Now Woody's friend and his wife appear on the screen. This woman is exactly the type suitable for me, thought Silverberg ruefully, as he did each time, he watched the film. The two are trying to find Woody a girlfriend. Despite Woody's frantic efforts, he fails to impress any of the dates he is fixed up with. I know the feeling, empathizes Silverberg, aware that nobody took the trouble to fix him up with a date because of the false assumption that he need only snap his fingers, or like Bogie, just whistle, and they would come a-running; yet like Woody, he struck-out similarly with the girls who really mattered to him. Yes, I know the feeling, he repeats as Woody continues to fail.

"Do you?" Silverberg feels Woody ask him, fixing him with a stare, a moment before the scene shifts to where Woody enters a bar with his blind date. Silverberg tenses, this is the scene in which that dude tries to muscle in on Woody's date. Woody wants to take the girl out of there and stands up to do so. The dude pushes Woody back into his chair. "Sit down," he says menacingly. Silverberg strains to keep from leaping at him with a bone-crushing tackle. Then, unable to restrain himself any longer, he hurtles toward the screen, sailing smack through it into Woody's seat, finding himself suddenly sitting in the bar in his place. The dude's eyes widen. Sitting next to him no longer is a skinny guy with glasses but a man packing 220 pounds of muscle. The dude stammers an apology and now it is his turn to stand up — to get away from a potentially bad scene. The blonde looks at him — Silverberg — in amazement.

Silverberg is no less amazed. Through the screen he sees Woody sitting in the seat in the movie theater which Silverberg himself had occupied only moments before.

Woody, too, is amazed, but recovers more quickly than Silverberg, maybe because he is lighter on his feet, maybe because he has been subjected to more abrupt scene changes in life, or maybe because he was brought up in New York and not Far Hills, Indiana. Woody looks relieved. "You came in the nick of time, boychik," he says.

Silverberg is speechless. The girl hangs on his arm adoringly. "It can't be," Silverberg says. "I love your movies, Woody... but to be in one... to be you ..."

"Mazel tov."

"What'll I do?"

"You've got a girl with her pretty pink tongue hanging out at the sight of you."

"But what do I do with Bogie?"

"Send him packing."

"Send Bogie packing? Bogie?"

The girl continues to look at him adoringly.

"You haven't got much time," Woody prompts him.

"What do you mean?"

"The film is running. You've got to run, too."

"But I'm a tackle, not a running back."

"If you want the girl, run!"

Woody stands up.

"Wait!"

Silverberg shouts in panic.

Woody raises a calming hand.

"Listen — what's your name?"

"Silverberg, sir."

"Look, Silverberg, I know you've seen my movies and admire me. Why else do I see you out there so many times?"

"Woody, I always wanted to talk with you about 'Zelig.'"

"Not now, not now."

"Yes, but…"

"Be me. Reduce a bit. Wear glasses. You can do it."

"Yeah… maybe I won't be a potential all-American tackle anymore. I'll be… you…"

"Right. And I'll be… " The seat-back cracks suddenly from the power of his hand which he has just placed upon it — "…you. I've got your strength!"

"And I feel weaker."

Woody scratches his head. "I guess I'll have to put on a few pounds."

Silverberg smiles.

"You'll like being a tackle. It's what you always wanted. And the girls."

"Wow, no longer the skinny kid on the beach with bullies throwing sand into my eyes. Now, I'll be the thrower…"

"But you'll have to work at it. I've got a tip for you."

"Anything that might help."

The blonde is rubbing against Silverberg — or what had been Silverberg.

"And Silverberg-ex, do something. That broad is about to rape you."

"What do I do?"

"Just hang on — to the film, not her. It'll take you with it."

And in truth Silverberg was already grasping at the rim perforations of the film as if it were an opposing halfback trying to slant off tackle, holding on to the now rapidly moving film for (what he hoped would be) dear life.

Extenuating Circumstances

Unlike the court which raised this aspect of the "alleged murder" committed by yours truly, I would refer to it as "justifiable homicide." Or maybe, "poetic justice." Let the reader be my judge.

No ordinary "murder," for sure. More, the "de-throning," as I like to think of it, of the diva — none other than Brenda Singer of enduring fame. Orange was her favorite color and now it is my unfavorable color as prison garb. Her revenge? I wouldn't put it past her.

My road to what I did and where I am now because of it began at an earlier age. My singing ability. You could say, my journey of a thousand miles began with a single note. By twelve months of age, I could imitate parts of songs sung to me by my parents, and by three years could carry a tune and sing with a steady rhythm. People (mostly relatives) said I was a born Judy Garland. I wonder now if they don't consider me the Wicked Witch of the East-Side. On the other hand, they used to brag that Louie Buchalter, head of Mafia hit squad, Murder Inc., was a far relative and so they might excuse me since "it runs in the family."

Later I was in the school choir and often a soloist. I won a number of amateur singing contests, took the lead in school musicals, graduated to singing in clubs, and appeared in Off-Broadway musicals, which led to my becoming the understudy for the diva, in the popular, long running, musical "Lovely Lady." This, I thought, would be my launch to stardom. I waited breathlessly for her to miss a performance so that I would take her place. It never came. For two years straight — the running time of the musical before it ended (with the diva's murder) — I waited. And waited. Never a cold or even or a weekend vacation on her part to give me my chance.

I began to believe the diva did it on purpose. That she was afraid I would eclipse her with my performance. That she wouldn't begrudge me even one night of fame. You would think a person with her singing reputation had nothing to fear. I would give one good performance, even a great performance, and the next day she would be back in the limelight. But no, she couldn't allow me that.

And so the idea which had seemed meshuga at first, grew on me, gnawed at me, kept me up at nights. I would injure her so that she couldn't appear. Enough of an injury to allow me to take her place for at least one night.

So why did you kill her? you ask. Hey, I'm a singer, not a perfect-injury planner. When I hit her with her

Grammy Award, I didn't think it would do her in. Perhaps I was so angry at her for her reluctance to give me a chance that I put too much effort into it. My mother used to claim that as a child my temper-tantrums were very physical. The diva slumped to the floor without emitting even a C-note.

Now, I was in trouble. Instead of clucking sympathetically at her "accident" (I hit her from behind) and when she regained consciousness, insisting I was admiring her Grammy when my butter fingers let it slip, and she rendered sufficiently unfit to appear (I pictured myself saying to her, "the show must go on"), I had to keep her body from being discovered before I could go on stage that night. I had come to her lavish apartment on a pretext (an autograph for my niece's album cover of the diva's latest hit album).

After murmuring a "zol lebn" (May she live), alas, followed by "olehusholem" (May she rest in peace), I went through a series of elaborate musings on how to get rid of her body so I wouldn't be discovered having murdered her. These included throwing her body into the Hudson, planting a false suicide note (because she feared she was losing her voice) and one so ridiculous I won't mention it here (hint: it involved a Starbucks — the diva was a coffee aficionado and boycotted the chain). Yet I knew I wasn't capable of pulling off any cockamamie scheme to get rid of the body. Instead of watching Tarantino movies, I had watched reruns of The Wizard of Oz.

An uncle later visited me in prison and lowered his voice so the guard wouldn't hear, "In this place Louie got the chair. You're lucky New York State did away with the death penalty." "I wasn't convicted of Murder One," I hissed back. "Too bad Louie was no longer among us to advise you about getting rid of the body." "Yeah, I would have rewarded him by starring in a musical based on his life. Then I wouldn't have had to worry about the critics panning the show." "You could call it 'Hello Louie!' my uncle beamed.

I hoped to get in one, maybe even two, performances and then "pay my debt to society" (and to her many fans). I knew I would become the hated bitch of the media. And so I became. When I entered prison, a large group of her fans was there to boo me in. I didn't say anything to the pestering media people — I was singer, not a politician, or Al Capone.

In fact, I did get in one performance but, alas, no rave reviews because the diva's body had been discovered just before the time of my performance (but too late to stop it) and before the reviews came out. The media was full of "the demise of the diva" and nothing else. This failure for recognition gave me a feeling worse than when I heard the judge pronounce my prison sentence. I hadn't counted on such a quick discovery of the diva's body. A peeping Tom across the street had seen her body when he came to do his annual evening voyeurism.

So now I'm in Sing Sing. Fitting, eh. Maybe I will write a book, a best-seller like that of the ice-skater who ruined the chances of a rival. They have asked me to sing in the annual prison musical. (Louie, wherever he is, would be pleased.) I told them I would think about it. I just hope my understudy, if I will have one, won't pull off a copy-cat murder. Or the diva's dybbuk (malicious soul of a dead person) take the place of my own.

The court didn't find any extenuating circumstances to help lower my sentence, but you, dear reader, are my Court of Last Resort.

The Memory Eraser

Let me tell you the way it happened. One day in November, two years ago it was, I was sitting outside the store, enjoying the nice weather, knowing winter was coming and I wouldn't have many more opportunities, when I saw him coming toward me. (This is looking back, since I didn't pay much attention to him then.) He looked to be around fifty, but something else about him caught my eye. Maybe the fact that, as he approached, he was looking at me closely. He stopped opposite me, and without a greeting said, "You got any bad memories you want to get rid of?"

After a moment of surprise, I decided to play along with him.

"Yeah, I have a few," I chuckled.

"I can get rid of them for you." His tone was serious.

"Really," I answered, pulling back in an exaggerated gesture of doubt. "You gonna lay hands on my noggin?"

"No," he said, "nothing like that. Nothing physical."

What caught me was his earnestness — so opposed to the weirdness of his claim . Besides, I've always been a sucker for the unusual. Maybe because of my work, which is rather boring, so that any diversion is welcome. Even a harmless nut case.

"You interested?" he persisted.

"Yeah, I'm interested," I said, standing up. "Come inside." I didn't want anybody to overhear this wacky conversation and I begin to think I was starting to lose it. It could hurt business. 'Ephraim's going soft in the head.' That kind of thing.

"I can do it here," he said.

"Inside," I repeated. "It sounds like an inside job."

His serious, even pained expression which seemed to be an integral part of him, broke into a brief, grudging smile, as if he had read my concerns. After he had followed me inside, I already regretted my invitation, wondering how I was going to get him outside again. I said to him, rather peremptorily," Ok, do your stuff."

"It'll cost you two hundred shekels."

I raised an eyebrow. "Not cheap."

He shrugged. "Any particular memory you'd like to part with?"

I thought for a few moments. "When I was in second grade, Nadav Golan spat on me. It doesn't sound like much, but…"

He nodded. "Give me the two hundred first."

"Why?"

"Because after you forget, you may deny that you ever had the memory."

I went to the cash register, took out a 200-shekel bill, and handed it to him. At the same time, I tried to stave off the feeling that I was a sucker, "If you fail to erase the memory do I get my money back?"

He smiled a wan smile. "I never fail."

He put the bill in an old wallet without counting it. Somehow that was a point in his favor. "Now think of Nadav —"

"Golan."

"— spitting on you."

I did so.

After some moments he asked, "Do you remember Nadav Golan spitting on you in the second grade?"

I looked at him blankly. "What are you talking about?"

"Your memory — you do remember that I erase memories."

"Yes, but…"

"You had a certain memory about a Nadav Golan. That was the memory you wanted to get rid of."

I must have looked doubtful because he took the two hundred shekel bill from his wallet. "You paid me these to get rid of a memory. That you remember."

I remembered. But still I was dubious. He noticed it and nodded slightly as if he was not surprised by my reaction. "You want me to prove it? I'm used to it."

"Yes, I do."

"Very well. We'll take another memory you want

to get rid of. Write it down, crumple up the paper into a ball, put it into your right hand, close your fist over it. After I have erased your memory, you can open your hand and read it. This time it's on the house. Take another memory you want to erase. But this time something you don't mind parting with. You're already sorry about Nadav Golan."

He was right. I had seemingly had some memory connected to a Nadav Golan that was apparently unpleasant, but still I felt as if I had lost something. Like a tongue that still searches for a hole in a tooth after it has been filled.

"It's common. People don't like to part with memories, no matter how bad."

"Ok, I cut myself shaving yesterday. I can part with that one without remorse."

"Write it down," he ordered.

I did so, crumpled the paper as he had suggested and put it inside my right fist.

"I see you cut yourself good. After I banish your memory, you can still feel the cut. Now think about cutting yourself shaving yesterday."

I did. When he reminded me that I had cut myself shaving yesterday, I did not remember. He instructed me to read the note in my hand. On it was written: "Yesterday I cut myself shaving."

A weird feeling came over me. "I simply do not remember."

"You have a cut on your chin to prove it."

I fingered my chin. He was right.

I was a believer.

"How do you do it?" I asked.

"I just have the person think about his memory. I concentrate on thinking about it at the same time. That's all there is to it."

From a believer, I rushed to become a disciple. "You can help people to forget traumatic things? Like people who survived the Holocaust?"

"Most people choose to hold on to their bad memories, no matter how bad. I guess they're too much a part of them to part with."

I thought about it for a while, about some of my painful memories. "Yeah, I think you're right about that."

We both were busy with our private thoughts until I broke the silence, "You were born with this — this ability."

"No."

"How did you acquire it?" I pressed him.

"I was mugged."

I thought he was kidding until he continued in a solemn voice as if it was a memory he would like to part with, "A man came up to me and suddenly hit me over the head with something hard and ran off with my wallet."

"And the blow gave you this ability?"

"Yes. I only discovered it gradually, but I trace it to the mugging."

"That reminds me of something I read once. I trot it out whenever I get caught up in discussions of 'What is art?' A true story of a French storekeeper who lived in the 19th century. Maybe I remember the story because I am a storekeeper. Anyhow, one day something fell off a shelf onto his head. From that day he began to write operas. He became a successful composer known all over France. Not as well-known as Bizet, but enjoying a considerable reputation. He wrote many operas and basked in his fame until one day he fell and received a blow on his head. From that day he was unable to write a note."

My listener's face took on an expression of wonder. "You mean…?"

"Why not? Another blow on your head might take away your power — if you want to part with it."

He fingered his chin thoughtfully, which amused me since I had done the same after he erased my memory, and also because it was the first sign of doubt I had seen him display since we met. "I don't know… I make a pretty good living. I'm not the type to go on the stage with it like those mind-readers or people who bend forks. Still, it's a unique talent. I don't know…"

"You haven't paid a price?"

An expression more pained than his usual one formed on his face. "Yes, oh yes. I've had my share of mockers. The doubting Thomases who don't give me a chance to prove my ability. Worse, my wife left me. She was afraid I would unconsciously rob her of her memory. It erases good memories, too. Also, she feared the thing itself. She saw me as a kind of sorcerer. And she said I had changed."

"And if you 'lost' your talent she would go back to you?"

His pained expression softened. "Yes, I think she might. She never remarried. I pass her in the neighborhood sometimes and she always asks me how I am doing. But that's the extent of it. If we had had children…"

"So, get somebody to hit you on the head," I half joked. "There are types around today who will kill for two hundred shekels. Get one to give you a slight concussion."

"I don't know."

"Your wife would take you back."

"Maybe… I think you're right… Yet… how can I put it. It's a curse — and yet it's special. I don't know…"

Suddenly, he grabbed my hand and shook it. "But still I thank you." His voice had lost some of its sadness. He started to leave, stopped, reached into his pocket and took out the two hundred bill I had given him. "Here, take the two hundred back."

"Why?" I asked.

"For the solution — or possible solution. In case I decide to try it."

"That's all right," I said. "It's been an interesting morning. In my time, believe me, I've paid more for less."

"No," he insisted, "this could be a big help. I'd appreciate it if you would take it. Fair is fair."

I took it. "But sign it for me."

He seemed pleased. He wrote his signature slowly, as if he were signing a painting. Or a will.

Today the same bill, framed in glass, hangs on the

wall. People think it was given to me by my first customer when the store opened. I didn't tell them its true history. So why did I hang it?

I guess I didn't want to forget him.

Sensual Android

Liebowitz lay naked next to this luscious woman. Ok, an android—but what an android! The latest model in sensual androids. Now he had the uncanny feeling that, like Socrates taught the art of love by Diotima, he was going to be taught how to make love by a specialist.

Prior to their entering the amorous bed, Vanessa had put on a music-pod of Rubenstein playing the 'Moonlight Sonata.' She then began to remove her metallic clothing; matter-of-factly, without any hint of embarrassment — unlike Liebowitz, who did so also, if most uncomfortably. She finished first. Liebowitz, to his considerable embarrassment, was briefly delayed by a stuck zipper. Vanessa feigned not to notice, though a slight movement of her nether lip betrayed her and Liebowitz thought he discerned the pale fire in her eyes suddenly go out. Waiting for him to finish undressing, Vanessa stood there in all her splendid nakedness.

Liebowitz began to gather his clothes from the bed where, in his unavailing haste, he had at first put them, with the purpose of laying each article of clothing neatly on the hanger which stood in the corner of the room. Vanessa, grasping his intention at once, arrested him, in a voice of impatience —- or was it disdain — and ordered him, "Throw them on the floor, Liebowitz." This caused him feel like the trembling human bridegroom with whom a vast gleaming bronze Aphrodite climbed off her plinth and slips into bed with, in a story of Prosper Merimee.

At this point, he kissed her, gingerly, tentatively. She kissed back with more force.

"Don't be bashful," Vanessa urged him.

Stop thinking so much, Liebowitz admonished himself. Concentrate. The success of the evening depends upon it. Hardly propitious was his suddenly recalling the admonition: "A man is not too old until it takes him longer to rest up than it did to get tired." But he was rescued from speculative philosophy as the physical requisites began to demand his total concentration. Already his pituitary gland was manufacturing a potent adreno-corticotrophic substance. At the same time his adrenal gland was stimulated, his blood pressure rose, there occurred a swift breakdown of his white blood cells, his pulse quickened, his circulation jumped and his heart action sped up. It had been a long time since his physiology had been subjected to such (pleasurable) stress. He sensed that no reciprocal physiology was taking place on the part of his partner, even though the outward manifestations of the act were taking place, to his considerable pleasure.

In the wall mirror, Liebowitz caught himself and Vanessa intertwined. 'The enraptured beast, doomed to one day die, as so many are' — Nabokov's gentle reminder. It applied to him, not to Vanessa. But then Nabokov had lived before the age of androids.

Although, on one hand, sex with Vanessa was pleasurable; on the other hand, it was marred with worries on the part of Liebowitz. Worries beyond the basic worry of whether he would succeed physically with this fabulous beauty. He sighed, reflecting, why were even his most intimate moments invariably accompanied by a flavoring of vile farce.

And after Liebowitz had "worked" and had more or less acquitted himself in his love-making with Vanessa, he felt exhausted, like a rooster after the hens have been serviced, yet immersed in the euphoria of successful release. Unlike his human partners, who often slept following the act, Vanessa seemed to be stimulated to speech — Liebowitz paying the price for having put so much intellectual input into her makeup. She was going on, a sound like the somewhat mechanical buzzing of bees in his ears.

He took the fingers of her right hand in his, a hand with her long tapering fingers so soft and yet powerful as a strangler's.

He bestowed a kiss on her neck. And there came to

him the words: 'Your neck is like David's tower built for an armory.'

The Song of Songs was also fitting for an android.

The Giant Shrimps are Coming. For Me, Benny Goldstein!

I read that a scientist recently wrote a book claiming that an artifact he observed in our solar system came from an earlier civilization far more advanced than ours. I accepted this possibility, though pride in our civilization took a hit. What I found less acceptable was the scientist's claim that aliens from this civilization have the form of man-sized shrimps.

Why did this theory panic me? First, let me say I prefer aliens which are humanoid in form, less threatening than, say, giant shrimps. But the real reason for my paranoia is the fact that before going exclusively kosher, I ate shrimps! Not only ate them, but enjoyed their in-shrimp-sauce shrimp cocktail taste.

What I fear is that the super-intelligent shrimp-formed aliens that are light years ahead of us in capabilities can read our minds, including our memories. More particularly, my mind and my memories. And even more particularly, my shrimp thoughts and memories. That they know that I ate — and enjoyed — eating shrimp.

My nightmare is that they may seek poetic retribution for my shrimp cuisine habits: eating me in their favorite man-sauce.

If alien giant shrimps are more powerful versions of earth shrimp, they could easily subdue me. Earth shrimp use their forelimbs like clubs and deliver blows so quickly and forcefully that pockets of seawater vaporize in explosions of light and heat. They pack a 50 miles-per-hour punch. Now giant shrimp would, accordingly, have much more power and would be able to pummel me without mercy. And since earth shrimp have powerful raptorials that are used to attack and kill prey either by spearing, stunning, or dismembering, their more deadly big brothers might choose to spear me just the way I speared my cocktail shrimp.

I have some, but not much, hope in the fact that in my memory from 1951 or so, are the words to the song, "Shrimp Boats." Its first four lines are:

Shrimp boats is a-comin'
Their sails are in sight,
Shrimp boats is a-comin'
There's dancing tonight!

Assuming they are not grammar pendants for civilization grammars, the giant shrimp might take this as a pro-shrimp sign on my part and forego any thoughts of ingesting me or otherwise seeking revenge for eating habits I have long since abandoned. I emphasize this in case they are reading my thoughts at this moment.

I also attempt to block out thoughts that shrimp are not kosher. Not kosher, that is, among Jews on the planet earth, without speculating whether the kosher laws apply to other planets or civilizations that existed millions or even billions of years before Jewish scripture and commentaries were written. If they have Talmudic scholars among them, they might want to take the latter into consideration.

Worse thought. Perhaps the aliens are actually lobster-shaped folk and they would discover that in my pre-kosher eating period, I also ate lobster! Perhaps they would wish to boil me before ingesting me!

My scientist's theories were inspired by his sighting an object he saw in the sky that led him to speculate it was junk from a more advanced civilization. He did not suggest, thank the stars, that it was a shrimp plate or other shrimp-related object which would have seemed to me a death knell for me, as it would tend to validate his alien-man-sized-shrimp conjectures and all that I fear because of my past-regrettable (if you are reading my thoughts, shrimp guys) ingesting habits.

Remember one man's or creature's eating habits are another's anathema. The quality of mercy is not strained on earth (whatever you folks strain, or don't). Not my original phrasing, a guy named Shakespeare — not comparable, of course, to your brilliant artists which surely use a lot of wonderful, positive shrimp metaphors and images, which if I knew any, would throw in here.

By the way, I am a small person in stature, a "shrimp" as the other kids called me, if that helps my cause. True they didn't use the term as a compliment, but I always accepted the term; especially in retrospect, as now, compared to you super-intelligent and merciful beings.

Hasidic Conundrum

I, Joshua Stein, have a friend, Aaron Greenberg, who is a full Hasid, unlike myself who am a ¼ Hasid or a ½ Hasid on good days.

Once Aaron was a non-Hasid like me. In fact, we were non-Hasids together, but that was many years ago, which makes his evolution (you should excuse the term) to being a Hasid today all the more impressive.

I got a phone call from him the other day (we are not in contact often now due to our Hasidism gap). He had some pants he wanted to make me a gift of. Apparently, he had received them from someone in a transaction whose intricacies bar it from being explicated. For some reason the pants weren't suitable for my friend, so he wanted to perform a mitzvah and make a gift of them to me. Or maybe they were suitable for him and he, nevertheless, wanted to make them a gift to me, thus magnifying the size of the mitzvah and raising him, at least in this matter, to a tzaddik (righteous one) — or at least a ½ tzaddik.

The truth is that I have too many pairs of pants already; my wife wants me to get rid of a goodly portion of them, there being no room for them in the closet. The thought crossed my mind that the pants were really his and his wife was complaining that he had too many and there was no room in his closet.. I immediately dismissed the thought; in the face of a mitzvah, I refused to harbor such a counter-mitzvah thought.

I did not want the pants — and yet how to refuse a mitzvah? For to refuse a mitzvah — to not allow one to be performed — is to ally oneself with the dark instead of the light.

There was only one ethical course of action — I would perform a transfer mitzvah. I agreed to take the pants, planning to make them a gift to someone else. My only problem was whether I had to tell my friend. I searched the Talmud but could not find a definitive answer. My wife, no mean Talmudist, was no more successful. I decided not to tell him in accordance with the tenet of Maimonides that declared anonymous charity as the highest form of charity. I immediately felt the warm glow of a ¾ Hasid.

The Nun and the Rabbi

Sounds like the beginning of a joke. And in some ways, it was. Dawn was the name of a blind date someone fixed me up with. "You'll like her —she's a bit nuts, like you." Which turned out to be true. For instance, on that first date, she told me that her great ambition in life was to parachute into the Ecuadorian jungle and convert the head-hunters to Christianity. Not something to impress a Jewish guy whose acquaintance with head-hunters was of the type that existed in the corporate world.

Dawn was devout in the evangelistic sense. Every other word from her enticing mouth was "Jesus." I felt like I was dating a country music singer. But Dawn turned out to possess a physical side to go with her spiritual side. It enabled me to suffer her religious fervor. She was amazing in the sack. I dubbed her "the contortionist." And that is why I kept dating her, disregarding the advice of someone: "Don't go to bed with anyone crazier than you are."

If Dawn was flexible physically, she was rigid spiritually. For instance, she kept trying to interest me in Jesus, "Jesus the Christian," she sometimes added. I told her that Jesus wasn't a Christian — he didn't worship himself — he was the founder of Christianity. I told her on that first date that I was Jewish, too, like Jesus, but she didn't want to hear it. I told her that his first followers were Jewish who, together with their Jewish brothers, rose up against the Roman oppressors and, with them, were wiped out, and that thereafter Christianity spread to countries outside the Land of Israel where it then lost its Jewish aspects. "You should have been a rabbi," she commented, seemingly unimpressed.

I would have continued to put up with her nudnik attempts at converting me for the sake of her non-spiritual virtues had not, alas, our relationship come to an end when she informed me that she searched for "more spirituality", and decided to stop being a Protestant and become a "Catholic nun"! I tried to dissuade her, including telling her she would be wasting her "exemplary physical demonstrations of love." No, she insisted, they might not accept her as a nun if her boyfriend was Jewish.

Dawn left to become a nun — "a bride of Jesus" to quote her. "Mazel tov," I congratulated her, and turned to the daunting task of trying to find a second Dawn. I wasn't a type for singles' bars. I wasn't even good at watching other guys succeed in singles' bars, I stayed on the outsides — on the fringes. I'm a fringe person.

The thing that saved me in trying to meet women in the past was the blind date. Even though when my blind date saw me, she would exclaim, "I wanted a date, not a fig," or behave toward me as if that's what she thought. I had so many blind dates that after five years, I found myself matched with the same dates I had had before. What hurt was that they didn't remember me. But then bingo! my blind dates finally paid off when I had the one with Dawn.

Perhaps subliminally affected by Dawn's spiritual searching or in shock from losing her, I decided to become a rabbi. A Reform rabbi.

I was ordained, given a congregation in Jersey and, being single, was urged to get married as that would be more suitable to the congregation's image of image of a rabbi. I did get married to a woman who indicated that she was interested in me but, alas, she wasn't Dawn, from the physical standpoint. That wasn't the only reason that we separated, but it was one of them. How did the Talmud put it: When they first married, they could sleep together in a bed narrow as a knife-blade; when the marriage fell apart, a bed wide as a meadow wasn't enough for them. Since we didn't have children, the divorce was arranged without too much wrangling. The congregation wasn't please, but I was not fired, maybe because nowadays there are gay and lesbian rabbis or maybe the fact that I "lightened up" my sermons with humorous inclusions made me popular with listeners. They dubbed me, "The Standup Rabbi" and "our Jackie Mason." Because of the show I put on, even non-Jews began to attend services. Dawn, by the way, had never been impressed by my humor. I learned quickly enough never to joke, even mildly, about Jesus. For instance, "How did Jesus brew tea?" "Hebrew it," resulted in a punishment of a week's celibacy. The closest she came to a Jesus joke herself was, "Jesus rose from the grave and you, you can't get out of bed," but probably she was being serious.

I thought more and more about Dawn. So much so that I thought about trying to find her and convince her to leave the convent and return to me. To gain access to her in the convent, I considered renting a priest's garb and even considered, momentarily, actually becoming a priest. This shows my nutty aspect was getting out of control.

Fortunately, before I spiraled completely out of control, I received an email from Dawn stating that she had abandoned being a nun after one of the nuns, an expert on the Talmud, either for the purpose of confirming biblical predictions about Jesus' being the Messiah, or perhaps to help in converting Jews, led Dawn to become fascinated with Judaism to the extent that she had converted to Judaism! And not only Judaism, but Orthodox Judaism. She added that if I would become Orthodox, we could renew our relationship "on a higher spiritual plane" and she hinted at possible marriage.

I replied simply that an Orthodox Jewish life wasn't for me, but perhaps we could compromise on a Conservative Jewish life style. I told her I was halfway there, since I was a Reform rabbi. She would hear none of it, hinted that I was in effect a goy, and thereafter refused to answer my emails.

After a time, I received an email from her telling me she had met a Yeshiva graduate "who looked a lot like you," married him, and they were going to emigrate to Israel, to live in "the Holy City of Jerusalem."

Fortunately, shortly thereafter, I met a girl who looked a lot like Dawn and also possessed some of her attributes. The congregation was pleased and offered to reward us with a honeymoon sabbatical year in Jerusalem, but I feared being too close to Dawn. Although my wife was a lot like Dawn, she wasn't a contortionist.

The Restaurant Michelin Missed

The restaurant's official name was "The Hole in the Wall," or was, perhaps, a sobriquet bestowed on it by those of us ate there. If you asked the owner/waiter about the origin of the name, he would answer, "What does it matter, it's the food that counts."

"The food" encompassed all six choices on the menu — if there had been a menu. Actually, four or five, depending on his mood. "Take it or leave it," he would invariably snarl.

You took it. Usually some combination of broccoli. We suspected spinach, especially when he would add, "You'll be strong, like Popeye." Louie's comments — someone said that was his name albeit that his customers never seemed to dare to be on a first-name basis with him — came at no extra cost. He was rumored to be an ex-Catskill resort comic; according to others, an ex-bouncer. Only from regular customers would he accept a hint of criticism. His response was always the same, "Accept misfortune as a blessing. Do you wish for perfect health, or a life without problems? What would you talk about?" we suspected Louie borrowed it from his Catskill *tummler* days.

Despite the décor (ok, Louie would scorn the word), principally, an ill-lit wallpaper featuring a — what — centaur? pattern, or you-guess-what, the poor lighting (Louie's "romantic atmosphere") encouraged the farer's imagination.

Though small, "Louie's" was invariably full to the extent of its limited space. Why did anyone frequent the restaurant, despite the "minus-one Michelin rating," as the wags denoted it. Quick service. For those who disdained frills, were put off by the bowing head-waiter/wine list/ "cuisine" restaurants shtick. Eat quick and acceptable fare — if you liked broccoli and similar. A restaurant, make that eatery, tailored for our text-message age. Not "new cuisine," not "old cuisine," "the same cuisine."

Oh, and Louie served alcohol — beer. Not Carlsbad and such. "Beer." We suspected the beer had been left over from prohibition days, (rumor had it that Louie was not above bootlegging in those days before he entered the restaurant business), when the barrels of beer sat off the 3-mile limit of the Jersey shore waiting to be spirited in by bootleggers.

If one sought wine, Louie would laugh, shake his head, and recommend you "go to the Four Seasons — it's

Spring (or whatever season it happened to be) and wine is in fashion."

I took my wife-to-be on our first (blind|) date there and she agreed afterwards to go on a second date with me. She passed my test for potential mates. And Louie had nudged me in the ribs (which I still felt the next day) with a "Not bad."

I knew I had a winner.

THE SIGN OF THE THREE

It began with a brief reference within that case I once had occasion to describe, *A Scandal in Bohemia*. At one point, Holmes had me look up the biography of Irene Adler, which (you may remember) was "sandwiched in between that of a Hebrew rabbi and that of a staff-commander who had written a monograph upon the deep-sea fishes."

The reference to the rabbi had aroused my curiosity, but I had to wait for an explanation until a good many years after Holmes had solved that case, when I came upon the reference to the "Hebrew rabbi" a second time.

"'Hebrew rabbi' is somewhat superfluous, Watson, as most rabbis are of that persuasion, but as I know that you often refer to my biographical lists, I ensure that the entries be as clear as possible."

"I am grateful for it, Holmes, yet what of his connection to you?"

"The connection began one afternoon at the very

place we find ourselves now, with a slow and heavy step upon the stairs and in the passage, a pause outside my door, followed by a loud and authoritative knock. I could tell by the authoritative knock that my visitor was a man. And it was my monograph, *A Study of the Influence of a Trade Upon the Form of the Hand* which served me well in this instance, for what struck me, Watson, upon his entry which I had bid him, was the thumb on his right hand. The skin above the first knuckle had been rubbed in a rightward direction. The opposite from the thumb of an English reader's turning a page. Clearly, my visitor read from right to left, and the language he read was probably Hebrew. 'You are a member of the Hebrew faith,' I said to him. In contrast to my usual client, the man was not astonished by my deductive skill. 'My head covering, my *yarmulke*, should reveal as much,' he chuckled."

I fixed the most perfect reasoning and observing machine that the world has seen with a stare. "I would have thought so, too, Holmes."

"Of course, but how many years have you known me, Watson. I invariably look at the shoes and hands of my visitors and form a conclusion identifying them before I take in their upper extremities. The *yarmulke*, as the skullcap worn by devout Jews is called, merely confirmed what I had already learned from my visitor's thumb. And, besides, I deduced he was a rabbi."

"How?" I asked, leaning forward, keenly interested, as always, in my friend's incisive reasoning.

"It was when I inquired of my visitor how I could help him. He replied, straightforwardly enough, 'I thought I could help *you*. Isn't that why I received a delivered note this morning addressed to Rabbi Goodman, bearing your signature, and requesting my assistance?' The rabbi was correct, Watson. I had forgotten that I had summoned him to assist me, since people knocking on my door usually come to me for assistance."

"How did it come about that you needed the help of a rabbi?"

"A most singular case required it. I call it, *The Sign of the Three*."

"How's that?" I said, remembering the singular affair of *The Sign of the Four*. I immediately inquired of Holmes if there was a connection with that case, the memory of which still causes a shiver to course up my spine.

"None whatsoever," Holmes calmed me, smiling that smile of his that indicated I was off the mark.

"The name, *The Sign of the Three*," Holmes elucidated, curling himself up in his chair with his knees drawn up, "was inspired by the Hebrew letter *shin*, which possesses three vertical protrusions."

I immediately complimented Holmes on his case's title, for I was struck at once by its aptness. "What does it mean, Holmes? — the *shin*?"

Holmes reddened slightly. "I confess, Watson, I did not know myself then that it was a *shin*. Which is why I called on the assistance of Rabbi Goodman."

"He of the rightward rubbed thumb?"

"Very good, Watson. In any event, my need of summoning the good rabbi came about because I was indeed perplexed. You remember *The Adventure of the Copper Beeches*, do you not?"

I affirmed as much.

"And you remember Miss Violet Hunter, the most exemplary protagonist thereof?"

I affirmed even more strongly.

"*The Sign of the Three* began with a visit by the same Miss Hunter, in some distress."

"I am sorry to hear of it, for she had a most forthright and upstanding character."

"So she had on the first occasion and, you will be pleased to know, so she had on the second. Upon removing her bonnet, I noted that her hair was still that luxuriant chestnut color, now long since restored to its pristine length. I inquired as to what problem brought her to Baker Street."

"'Oh, not mine, sir. That of my mistress.' She proceeded to explain in that clear manner of exposition of hers that she was employed by a good and kind woman, a Madam Rothschild, widowed, a distant relation of the eminent family, as governess to her niece, who lived with her. One day madam Rothschild had received a curious note slipped under her door. The note was undated and without the address of the sender.

Dear Madam [it said]
Your niece is the recipient
Of a substantial income.

I will be in further
Contact in due course.
W

"This was indeed a mystery," I remarked, breaking in, however reluctantly, into Holmes' narrative. "What did you imagine, my dear Holmes, that it meant?"

"I did not imagine, Watson. I brought my mind to bear upon the facts as I received them and proceeded from there."

"Quite so. And there was no further contact by the unknown benefactor?"

"The same question I put to Miss Hunter. 'None whatsoever,' she replied. Upon my inquiring if her employer knew anyone whose name began with the letter W, Miss hunter confessed to making a similar inquiry."

"I always considered that Miss Hunter would make an excellent, ah, accomplice to a detective."

Holmes chose to ignore my comment and continued with his narrative. "Madam Rothschild could think of no one whose name began with a W, save a Mr. Weinstein, a diamond cutter. She was too discreet to wish to inquire of Weinstein if he were somehow connected with the affair, and Miss Hunter, knowing to whom to turn in such cases, spoke of me, and her employer agreed. I paid a visit to Weinstein. My inquiries proved to be a cul-de-sac. He was not the benefactor."

"So you lacked any basis for clearing up the mystery."

"I immediately returned to my premises at Baker Street to mull over the matter. I came to the conclusion that the W might very well stand for Wellington, of the famous boot-making firm. The firm supplied boots to the Rothschild family. Perhaps Wellington also had contact with their less wealthy relative, Miss hunter's employer, or her niece. The next day I disguised myself as a wealthy Swiss boot importer and proceeded to the Wellington emporium, but soon discovered that Wellington was not the benefactor. Clearly, I was on the wrong track. I decided the answer must lie in the note itself."

Here, Holmes interrupted his narrative and showed me the note which he had kept all these years in his scrapbook. He took out his magnifying glass and magnified a portion of the note. "You see those fibers, Watson, they indicate a kind of fiber, not dissimilar to papyrus, only made in the near East. Having identified the fiber, I turned my attention to the W. It seemed a most singular W, not at all like a W written by an Englishman. Note the indentation on the right side, and the less indented left side — clearly it was written from right to left. Perhaps by a Hebrew writer. I sent for Rabbi Goodman, as I have already related, who confirmed, indeed, that it had been written from right to left, but that it was not an English W, but a Hebrew letter."

"The *shin*!"

"Excellent, Watson."

"With his piece of information, I visited Madam Rothschild. After the customary introductions, I inquired whether the *shin* suggested anyone. She meditated for some moments before remembering one Sheinblum, a distant relative, who had frequented a number of ports in his duties as a sailor. 'Had he any contact with the Near East?' I asked her. 'Why, yes, he resided for some years in the Holy Land."

"The source of the notepaper."

"Indeed, the source, Watson. Also, the source of the *shin*, the initial of Sheinblum's name in Hebrew, a letter he used as a signature initial in the Holy Land, and never thereafter abandoned for those subliminal reasons in all of us, Watson, that manifest characteristics that to others seem odd or inexplicable, but to ourselves are most rational. Upon my visiting Sheinblum, who possessed that genial, if taciturn, nature sometimes observed in men of the sea, he confirmed his intention to bestow a generous sum upon the niece, but had been ill for some months, a result of a recurrence of malaria contacted years before as a seaman on the England-Malaya trade route. As a result of a fray with Malay pirates, in which he distinguished himself, he had lost a leg. I had been advised of the fact by Madam Rothschild, upon my careful inquiry as to the characteristics of this then putative benefactor. He had, fortuitously, recovered from his relapse, and immediately made good the promised sum. There was therefore no need to pay him a return visit, which was a bit of a disappointment, as —"

"You had planned to employ a sailor's disguise, complete to a wooden leg."

"Capital, Watson, "exclaimed Holmes, clapping me on the shoulder.

Benkei Versus the Giant Carp

According to Japanese legend, the heroic samurai Benkei killed a giant carp which had swallowed his mother when she fell into a waterfall, which calls to mind the Japanese saying, apparently borrowed from the Yiddish, "If a person is destined to drown, he will drown in a spoonful of water," but then Benkei's mother did not do things half way. In any event, Benkei's mother escaped such a fate when the giant carp swallowed her, which almost caused Benkei to lose his taste for gefilte fish. In order to save his mother, Benkei knew he had to kill the giant carp.

Benkei had to defeat the giant carp not only to save his mother, but also in order to escape his having to commit seppuku, an act which would please no one except his mother-in-law. The same who dared to claim that sushi was tastier than gefilte fish. Of her it was written, "A nasty tongue is worse than a wicked hand," although she was adept at both. She forced Benkei to violate the sage advice that "Only one who can swallow an insult is a man;" albeit, he justified his refusal to do so on the basis, "The person who is his own master cannot tolerate another boss."

Facing the giant carp, Benkei concentrated on entering the state where his body and the sword he held become one — the oneness in which he was the sword and the sword was he: the state of MUGA, 'no ego' or 'no mind.' He thus achieved HONSHIN, 'the original mind' and SHIJIN, 'the perfect man,' and, more importantly, AI-UCHI 'free from the fear of death.' And, finally, ICHINEN, 'the instant in finding oneself standing sword in hand before the fallen enemy.'

Benkei killed the carp with one stroke of his sword. Now he had to act quickly to save his mother, violating the ancient proverb: "When your enemy falls, don't rejoice, but don't pick him up either," which was ok if your mother wasn't inside the enemy. Benkei picked up the giant carp and wrestled it onto the kitchen table. He beamed at his wife, "A year's supply of gefilte fish, go and have delivered a barrel of horse radish." Benkei then cut open the carp with his sword. Fortunately, his mother was still alive. "Nu, what are you waiting for," she said, "Get me out of this fish. I'm swearing off gefilte fish for life!"

Benkei nodded and pulled her out of the fish. "Do you mean, mother, you will substitute sushi?"

"Are you crazy, that would be admitting that your mother-in-law has better taste than me!"

There are those who claim that the legend of Benkei and the giant carp resulted when a Lost Tribe of Israel arrived in Japan — likely the tribe of Zebulun, seafarers who surely fished. (Moses: "They shall partake of the abundance of the seas"). The biblical Job asks, "Can you pull in leviathan with a hook?" Leviathan was a sea serpent that the righteous would dine on at the end of days. Perhaps the origin of the carp that transforms into a dragon. The kabbalist book, the Zohar, claims that the feast on leviathan is not literal but symbolizes the reception of enlightenment. The search for enlightenment is a basic tenet of Zen.

Benkei was no slouch when it came to looking for enlightenment. He rejected, as not applying to him, the statement, "Everyone wants to get enlightened but nobody wants to change." He was Japanese, and Zen stressed the search for enlightenment without having to wait for the end of days. Samurais, unlike the Jews, weren't known for their patience, the latter guided by the ancient tempo, "If it goes, it goes, don't force it." Having achieved the physical by killing the giant carp, Benkei was ready for the spirituality of Zen. In his search for enlightenment, he came across the Zen wisdom:

> You and I sip a cup of tea. That act
> is apparently alike to us both,
> but who can tell what a wide gap
> there is subjectively between
> your drinking and my drinking?
> In your drinking there may be no Zen,
> while mine is brimful of it.
> If it turns out that Zen adherents drink their tea

through a lump sugar in the manner of East European Jews who put a small piece of sugar between their front teeth and sip hot tea through it, there is, indeed, basis for the claim that a Lost Tribe of Israel reached Japan and influenced the traditional tale of Benkei and the giant carp.

For the rest of his life, Benkei adopted a positive outlook guided by the fear that "If the heart is bitter, sugar in the mouth won't help" while mindful of the Zen admonition, "Enlightenment is the food that eats you."

Gefilte? he mused, mindful of the giant carp that had swallowed his mother. Certainly stuffed.

A Golem for Me

Why did I build a golem?

Because a good (human) man is hard to find. Harder when you reach thirty-five. Yes, a young lady of 35, if that constitutes a young lady. A point where worries turn to panic. I was fed up with all the flesh fetishers and nudnik nerds that had panoplied my life. I felt like I was in a movie written by Nora Ephron, though she never had to build a golem because she was married three times.

I started to research how to build a golem. I knew zilch about building a golem. Only how to meet them. A joke this. Incidentally, some of my swains rejected me because they claimed my sense of humor was too "superficial." They preferred "Seinfeld" and "Friends" over Amy Schumer.

I boned up on golem historiography. The Golem of Prague was created in the 16th century by Rabbi Loew who created a golem out of clay from the banks of the Vltava

River. Others before him had tried to create golems. Two rabbis tried their hands but only managed to produce a very small calf, which they ate. I wouldn't want to create a golem calf. I'm a veggie. Became a vegetarian cause I thought it would help me to meet the right guy in a veggie-support group. At meetings we ate organic seaweed. I couldn't get the green off my teeth for two days afterward. Rabbi Shlomo ben Gabriol created a woman golem, apparently to do housework in the days before robot vacuum cleaners.

My golem would be without excessive body hair — my last loser was hirsute. I do not subscribe to the thesis that cavemen were the sexiest men in history. My hairy guy was not a problem in itself, but given his other personality attributes, I associate it with him. And my golem would not be bald. A balding loser in my past was obsessive about my hair — wanted it worn always long. He would move his chubby fingers in, thru, and under my hair, murmuring "Delilah." In short, a long-hair fetisher. Maybe because he wasn't able to tie it in a Samurai-style knot, then the fashion among men approaching middle-age. Another guy's hair was done up in dreadlocks, in his case well-named as I dreaded to see his locks after my first glimpse of them. He looked like somebody threw a plate of spaghetti over him. He failed to grasp my opening remark, "Where's the parmigiano?" I followed it up by mocking him as "My Medusa." He didn't have a clue. No, he wanted me to be his permanent dreadlocks braider. Said his last ditched him because of his hair. Now you understand why I preferred to create my own soul mate, assuming a golem has a soul. Hopefully, mine would.

In some versions of the legend, the golem was made of mud, not clay. In Cynthia Ozick's novel, a woman creates a female golem out of the dirt of her flowerpots. Because of my childhood trauma resulting from getting poison-ivy every summer, I avoided plants of any type. Clay was less messy to work with. Clay reminds me of Clay Epstein, a would-be suitor who lived up to his first name, and though he was, briefly, putty in my hands, he may have been the subconscious inspiration for my idea to build a golem.

Enough of golemic history. It was time for me to get to work on my baby. I took a Barbie male doll (one can hope) and a butter knife and Play-Doh and began to mold a clay imitation the size of a man. Ok, he didn't look like the Barbie doll, closer to the Golem of Prague but still an improvement on my dates. I repeated some incantations, variations of "Arise, Golem," and "Come to me, baby," and the protective incantation "You may be bigger, but I'm smarter."

To my amazement, the clay started to smoke (I stopped smoking, finally, two years ago) and to heat dull red (like my lipstick shade, "Indigo Rouge."), then a brighter red ("Blatant Cherry"), then cooling, turned an orange color ("Tangerine Joy'), and then dulled to something close to skin color. Clay had become flesh. The man then sprouted hair and a nose, eyes, lips.

I was proud of myself. Love at first sight? Not at

my age, but it/he definitely had possibilities. I planted a kiss on its cool lips. The chest of the golem started to heave slowly. Not with desire, with life. His lips parted and a deep sigh issued from him. The eyes opened, at first unseeing, then seeing. Me. He stared at me blankly. I seized the opportunity and pirouetted to give him the benefit of my still lithe (relatively speaking) form.

As he was naked, I decided to test him further. I became naked. The golem did not react. Nu, I said, taking his hand and putting it on my breast. He removed it as if it had touched a flame. I gave him another kiss, more French than the first one. His face took on a frightened look.

Miffed, I told him that I wasn't proposing marriage.

His visage took on a puzzled expression.

I was patient with him, a quality I had developed over the years on countless blind dates. Slowly he came around and we reached a modus vivendi. But his face I hadn't sculpted very well. In my ceramics class face-mugs were my weakness. My teacher complained that I was hopeless. I think he said that because I resisted his efforts to mold me. My golem's face made me feel like the Bride of Frankenstein, like in the old movie. His personality turned out to be better than ninety percent of my dates, but I couldn't look at him over my breakfast frozen yogurt without feeling I was about to vomit. Reluctantly, I had to destroy him, or it, since "it" wasn't exactly a "he" yet. Actually, I didn't have to destroy him, he destroyed himself when I began to sing to him, "Killing Me Softly". I have a terrible singing voice, am persona non grata at karaoke groups. In the school choir I was forbidden to sing. I had to mouth everything; they simply needed bodies. Which brings me back to the golem. By the time I finished the first three lines of "Killing Me Softly", he was ashes to ashes.

My second golem was more promising. But he had an obsession. He wanted to teach me Yiddish. I am bad at languages. One of my "hopefuls" (the guy, not the golem) was a linguist. In the end, we didn't speak the same language. This second golem actually rejected me. He began to rain Yiddish curses on me when I refused to learn Yiddish. The shayna maidel ("pretty girl") stage was over. He had the chutzpah to call me a golem. That did it. I finished him off by singing, "Killing Me Softly", which caused him to collapse on the floor, writhing in torment briefly before he turned to ashes. As it was Winter, I thought about using him on the front steps to prevent me from slipping on the ice. But it seemed somehow irreverent. I poured him down the garbage disposal.

Third golem. Bingo! He looked like Brad Pitt on a bad day, but still better than my past dates on a good day. And he liked me from moment one. Called me "Esther" and began praising me with quotations from the Song of Songs. I knew he was the one. We were married. He amazed the rabbi with his knowledge of the wedding ceremony and even more with his breaking the glass with his foot into splinters. "Samson," the rabbi beamed. He carried me over the threshold as if I was a feather, but when he wanted to honeymoon in Prague, I began to worry.

A Cake for Mr. Buchalter

Mr. Buchalter is what we always called him, my wife Leah and I, even when not in his presence. My wife's cousin. His full name was Lewis "Lepke" Buchalter ("little Louis" in Yiddish), which is what his mother called him, Later "Lepke Buchalter." Yes, he of Murder Incorporated, more commonly known as Murder Inc. We never used that designation, of course.

I wasn't crazy about Leah's cousin, but she insisted, "A nogoodnik, but mispicha is mispicha" ("family" in Yiddish). "Besides," she never failed to add, 'You don't want to be on his wrong side." "Also, his brother is a rabbi," she chose what she considered a point in his favor.

"The white sheep of the family," I ventured.

She stuck her tongue out at me.

Once, Leah asked me, if I had known who her famous (her word, I would have chosen "notorious") cousin was, would I have married her. "Well," I said after a pregnant moment's silence, "it is somewhat offputting."

I quickly added, "On the other hand, if somebody got on my nerves, he might be useful." In truth, I didn't know how I would have reacted. Dubious cousin or not, no one could bake cakes like Leah.

Which is why she called on me to deliver a honey cake to Buchalter "before shabbat (the sabbath)"

I swallowed. "Me? To Mr. Buchalter? Why the gift?"

"Not a gift. A request," she corrected. "From Mr. Buchalter."

It was an offer we couldn't refuse.

"Couldn't you send it by a delivery service?"

"He would be insulted. He's touchy. He likes the personal touch. Besides, he always gives generous gifts at our simchas (celebrations). Think of it as a small payback." Here she added, "It is written, 'The giver benefits as much as the taker.'"

And so I found myself carrying, gingerly, a box of honey cake to Buchalter. He didn't live far away.

There was a guard outside the entrance. Martin "Buggsy" Goldstein of notorious fame. He looked me over, looking for holster bulges, I presumed. He didn't frisk me. One look probably told him I was harmless. Or maybe he remembered me from a family function attended by Buchalter when he, Goldstein, was on guard duty.

I felt like I was in a Tarantino movie.

"Open the box," he ordered.

I complied. He looked at the contents. "Ain't got a saw in the cake?" he guffawed at his own joke.

I smiled, unable to fake a generous laugh at his side-splitter.

He waved me inside. I couldn't stifle the thought: How many people had that hand done away with?

I walked the long corridor to Buchalter's living room carefully, so as to not drop the cake. Now I knew how murderers doomed to 'walk the last mile' felt. Buchalter was a likely candidate for such a walk but maybe his cockiness banished the thought.

Inside, Buchalter was holding court with his coterie. A living tableau of a rogues' gallery or post-office wanted list. To wit: Harry "Pittsburgh Phil" Strauss, Abe "Kid Twist" Reles, and Albert "The Mad Hatter" Anastasia (on this occasion bereft of hat). Buchalter's branch of Murder Incorporated was interdenominational, if mostly kosher.

They all looked me over from top to bottom and bottom to top. I smiled weakly (I like to think of it as "gamely").

Buchalter greeted me. 'What's in the box?"

"Leah's honey cake. A gift"

"Jesus said, 'It is more blessed to give than to receive,'" declared Albert "The Mad Hatter" Anastasia.

"Not when it comes to my Leahaleh's cakes," corrected Buchalter. "Put it on the table, Sidney."

Despite my nervousness, I was pleased he remembered my name.

The table was close, but not close enough. I was so intent on not dropping the honey cake, that I dropped it.

The fact that I was inwardly nervous when I was in close contact with Buchalter was surely a factor.

I froze.

The group regarded the cake, half in the box, half sprawled on the floor. They looked at Buhcalter. They knew he had a short fuse. I knew he had a short fuse. A lot of guys in the next world knew he had a short fuse. Even as I faced him, my back flinched, as if it awaited a bullet. My life passed before me in fast forward.

"Oi," I stammered.

"Oi vey," Buchalter answered.

What kind of "Oi vey? Fortunately, he then laughed, amused rather than riled. "Leymene hent," (Butterfingers), he admonished me. "Klutz," chimed in Abe "Kid Twist Reles. Albert "The Mad Hatter" Anastasia said something in Italian. I doubted that it was complimentary. "Pre-cut," Buchalter added, which brought forth a laugh from the others.

I smiled weakly, a smile of relief. "I will gather it," I ventured.

'Nope," said Buchalter. "Leahlah's honey cake deserves the best. I'll take care of it, personally."

He picked it up and put it on the table. "More intact than O'Malley," he pronounced.

Apparently, the late O'Malley was a victim.

The others laughed, appreciating the in-joke.

Buchalter swiped at the honey cake with a finger, and then licked it. "Just proves Buchalter can have his cake and eat it. You guys are welcome to join me in an oneg shabbat (joy of the sabbath). You, too, Sidney," he added, pointing his trigger finger at me.

I thanked him and said I wanted to be able to attend synagogue before shabbat.

He nodded. "My brother, the rabbi, would approve. Thank the missus."

"I will," I promised.

"Sidney, take a piece of cake and on your way out give it to Buggsy."

I tried to keep my hand steady as I cut a generous piece and put it on a paper plate.

Harry "Pittsburgh Phil" Strauss bowed me out with an exaggerated bow.

Goldstein took the cake. "Pal. Can you hold my gat while I ingest."

I took the gun gingerly and careful to keep my finger far from the trigger, waited for him to finish. I hoped a rival gang wouldn't choose that moment to make a hit. Fortunately, Buggsy was a quick, if not fastidious, eater. He took back his gun in exchange for the paper plate for me to throw away.

At synagogue, where Buchtaler's brother was the rabbi, I said the prayer recited in gratitude when one is saved from serious injury or worse.

A Good Day for Nudnik Fish

I prefer my Tel Aviv from the days before the arrival of the glitzy marina. I berth my skiff wherever I find a bit of sand on the shore that hasn't yet been taken for private development. Nobody disturbs the boat — it's been around so long they know it's mine — vintage, like me.

Usually it takes me a while to catch the first fish. But that day as I sat in the skiff on the sea, they simply weren't biting. Changing bait, changing fishing spots — gornisht. "Can you pull in the leviathan with a fishhook?" asks Job. I would settle for a fish far smaller than leviathan, I mused — and then the fish jumped into the boat. I pounced on him before he could jump out of the boat. "Wait long enough and they come to you," I shouted triumphantly the old fisherman's wisdom.

He turned out to be a disappointingly small fish, though a pretty one — a type I had never seen before — with gold scales that put those of your aquarium goldfish in the shade. I picked him up to toss him back. He was too small for frying.

"Don't do that," the fish pleaded. "Not before using your three wishes."

A talking fish. Trouble. If you tell people a talking fish jumped into your boat, even bait-sellers will give you the fish eye.

"I thought that was a goyishe legend," I told him.

"Not in your case, he said.

I was in a bad mood since I hadn't caught any fish that Molly, my 'life partner' for the last two years of my life, could fry up. Molly traditionally threatened me before I went fishing to brain me with the skillet if I failed to bring back fish to fry. She never did but her biting comments if I didn't made me smart. In short, I lacked patience even for a reverse-schnorrer. "Get off my back," I growled at him.

"That doesn't count as a wish since your 'I'm not on your back' is a metaphor. Precise phrasing is all-important."

His chutzpah earned him a juicy Yiddish curse.

To my surprise, he replied in Yiddish: "A fool shows his annoyance at once, but a prudent man overlooks an insult." After a pause, "Ditto a prudent fish."

That he knew Yiddish mollified me. He seized on my softening, and said, again in Yiddish: "Nu, when fortune calls, offer her a chair."

I countered with: "If you have nothing to lose, you can try anything."

I vaguely remembered a bubbe meiseh about a fish

and three wishes which I was told as a child. "I have three wishes before you get your tuchas out of my boat? Is that it?"

"Essentially, yes. Although your somewhat synoptic version leans toward the pre-modern era of legends. The traditional 'magic fish' was somewhat cruel. We contemporary piscatorial wish-granters are a different breed. We see psychiatrists. We suffer guilt. If I jumped out of the boat without granting you three wishes, I would suffer angst and have to sit through too many sessions of remedial therapy. In short, you are the beneficiary of three wishes."

On the ropes from his spiel, and worried about Molly's reaction to my not catching a fish, I mumbled, "I wish I had a good eating fish to bring to Molly."

Suddenly the biggest mackerel I had ever seen was lying in the bottom of the boat.

"Sorry," said the golden fish. Not to me, to the mackerel. "I'm only a conduit. The legend, you know."

With the last of his strength, the mackerel nodded, sadly it seemed to me.

"Live in water, die on land," my fish tried to ease his passing.

This wish business actually worked. Too bad I wasted a wish on the mackerel, though he was mouth-wateringly meaty. Must have weighed fifty pounds, at least. My 30 pound test would have snapped with this hombre. Still I had two big wishes to use.

"How long have I got?" I asked the golden fish.

"To use your wishes?"

"Yeah. Not 'til I turn belly up."

The fish frowned, maybe disturbed by my dead fish… metaphor. "There is no statute of limitations — no time limit. But you could give some thought to me. I cannot complete the carrying out of my task until you use your last two wishes."

"You jumped into my boat, I didn't jump into yours."

"I am not authorized to go into the reasons for the form and purpose of our meeting. Let us say that the fact that you always toss back undersized fish and remove the hook gently out of the fishes mouths have not gone unnoticed."

With all the gab, I didn't notice the wind spring up and the water turn rough. Before I knew it a storm bore down on the boat. And of the three of us in the boat I was most at risk. I was a poor swimmer. "If a man is destined to drown, he will drown even in a spoonful of water," I reminded myself. My companions didn't have a problem. I looked up at the rain coming down in sheets. The words of the song, 'Fisherman on a Cold Wet Day,' came to me:

Every fishing rod has two ends

At each end, the wish to live

There only remains the need to know

Which of the two will live

The boat was filling up with water. "I wish I was back on terra firma," I murmured.

I was. I slapped my forehead with the palm of my hand. Wish number two — gone. When you fish alone you talk to yourself. I had long since given up on trying to get Molly to come fishing with me. "Together with you in a two room apartment is more than enough," she would say. Or "Your dinghy is not my idea of a Love Boat." For some time Molly had been urging me to take her on a cruise, but what good was sitting on a big boat if you couldn't fish from it. When I told her that, she refused to talk to me for a week. The adage admonishes, "Show her the tiller, but don't let her steer the boat." I knew better than to show Molly the tiller, let alone let her steer the boat.

I schlepped home the mackerel tightly gripped under my arm. In the other hand I carried the golden fish in a bait jar of water. I feared he might try to jump out, head for a sewer or something, but the golden fish, who could read thoughts as well as grant wishes, raised slightly a cautionary dorsal fin. "I'm under contractual obligation to you."

"Until the third wish is granted."

"Precisely."

Soaked to the skin, I headed for the modest apartment which I shared with Molly, who I met working behind the counter in 'Fish Tackle for Your Mackerel'. Molly claimed she had nothing to do with the name, but it smacked of the style of one, who, in her words, "tried her hand" at poetry and liked to read books.

When I kidded her that she was named for a tropical fish, she would say she identified with a Molly Bloom from a book. "Why her?" I asked.

"She made do with the men in her life," she replied. Molly was a cynic. Not someone that you came to with a tale about three wishes.

How did Molly end up with me? "I reeled him in, so to speak," she would tell anyone who asked how we met, and then explain how we met in the 'Fish Tackle.' She usually added, "My ex was a falafel seller. He called himself 'The King of Falafel' — I was the Queen — but I was getting too fat… on fish you don't get too fat." This last a bow in my direction. Yet despite her cynicism, Molly was enough for me. There's nothing lonelier than being a long-divorced man living in a cramped apartment without a woman.

On the way, I fantasized on which wish I would use my last wish. I considered wishing for another woman, younger and prettier and gentler than Molly. But then I told myself, You're used to Molly. Best not to fish in troubled waters. No, I would not use the wish to wish for something for me alone. I would wish for something for Molly and me, if that was permitted.

"Permitted if you phrase the wish jointly; that is, collectively; that is —"

"I wish you would stop with the legalese," I cut him short. Human lawyers were more than enough, I didn't like to have a fish lay down the law for me.

"Easily done!" he said joyfully. "And that is your third—and need I add, last — wish."

"You did that on purpose!" I thundered.

"Well within the parameters of the legend," he said

before he disappeared in a golden flash. Zie ga zink (go in good health), I said under my breath.

I resolved not to tell Molly or anyone else about all this. I'll just give her the mackerel. We'll dine off it for a month, at least. Some would say a wasted wish, but they won't have tasted it. And Molly will stop threatening to leave — at least for a month.

Kornfein

Kornfein lay naked next to this luscious woman. He found it hard to believe, especially after so many years of celebrating his celibate bed. Before he met his ex-wife, Sandra. he had not been confident with women, had only slept with one woman, and one time only.

Now he had the uncanny feeling that, like Socrates taught the ars amoris by Diotima, he was going to be taught how to make love by a specialist; this tantalizing possibility was immediately dampened by the thought (from where?) that "love takes up more space in the mind than it does in the bed"; which was followed by the yet more disconcerting thought (Levenstein's shade at work again?): "they sleep three in a bed."

Whimsically, Kornfein wondered if Cynthia thought she could become more intelligent by going to bed with him — the Love Goddess joined to the Great Mind — but then, with a certain frisson, he remembered that she had gone to bed with her late husband, Levenstein, the known literary critic — to whom Kornfein had labored as his assistant and in his shadow — no less a 'Great mind' than himself. Kornfein tried not to picture Levenstein and Cynthia in a sexual context. He could picture Levenstein sexually aroused only by intense literary discussion. And then he remembered, with a pang, that Sandra had once said something to the same effect about him! He strove to recall if her tone had been jocular or serious.

Prior to their entering the amorous bed, Cynthia had closed the curtains and then put on a disc, 'Moonlight Sonata,' played on the piano by Rubenstein.

Cynthia removed her clothing; matter-of-factly, without any hint of embarrassment — unlike Kornfein who did so also, if most uncomfortably. She finished first. Kornfein, to his considerable embarrassment, was briefly delayed by a stuck zipper — he felt himself an actor in a Yiddish comedy; Cynthia feigned not to notice, though a slight movement of her nether lip betrayed her and Kornfein thought he discerned the pale fire in her eyes suddenly go out. Seeing Cynthia standing naked in all her splendor, in comparison to his own poor naked form in comparison, Kornfein remembered Lacan's query whether the phallus is still a master signifier in the present order of Western society.

He began to gather his clothes from the bed where, in his unavailing haste, he had at first put them, with the purpose of laying each article of clothing neatly on the wooden hanger which stood in the corner of the room. Cynthia, grasping his intention, arrested him, in a voice of impatience, or was it disdain, "Throw them on the floor, Kornfein."

He recalled Sandra's once characterizing him as "cautious to the point of self-parody."

His hesitation apparently got on her nerves.

"Nu? What are you waiting for?"

"Godot," he didn't reply.

Above the bed a copy of Botticelli's painting 'The Birth of Venus.' He wondered if Cynthia identified with the Greek goddess of the painting. According to the myth, Aphrodite (another name for Venus), the goddess of love, was born from the foam produced when Cronus threw Uranus's genitals into the sea. This followed Cronus's using a scimitar to remove the testicles of Uranus, at Gaes's urging of vengeance against him. The Greeks didn't pussyfoot around when it came to sex. Kornfein considered edifying Cynthia with the Greek myth, yet feared she might consider it gauche, especially if he included the scimitar part, although Gaes's vengeful nature might strike a chord with her.

At this point Cynthia stamped her foot, perhaps, Kornfein conjectured, miffed at what she considered a delay in their proceedings. Cynthia's feet, Kornfein noticed, were long and large, unlike Sandra's petite wide feet. Kornfein, of course, forbore from informing Cynthia of this comparison. Instead, he kissed her, gingerly, tentatively. She kissed back with more force.

Above her, out of the corner of his eye, Venus was being born.

"Shem zikh nit," (Don't be bashful), Cynthia urged him.

Stop thinking so much, Kornfein admonished himself. Concentrate. The success of the evening depends upon it. Hardly propitious was his suddenly recalling the admonition: "A man is not too old until it takes him longer to rest up than it did to get tired." As counterpoint, he recalled the Yiddish saying: Az men lebt derlept men ("If you live long enough, anything can happen").But he was rescued from speculative philosophy as the physical requisites began to demand his total concentration. Already his pituitary gland was manufacturing a potent adrino-corticotrophic substance. At the same time his adrenal gland was stimulated, his blood pressure rose, there occurred a swift breakdown of his white blood cells, his pulse quickened, his circulation jumped and his heart action sped up. It had been a long time since his physiology had been subjected to such (pleasurable) stress. He had the odd sensation that no reciprocal physiology was taking place on the part of his partner, even though the outward manifestations of the act were taking place.

In the wall mirror, Kornfein caught himself and Cynthia intertwined. 'The enraptured beast, doomed to one day die, as so many are.' No time now for Nabokov's gentle reminder.

Although on one hand (after so many years of being without the commodity) sex with Cynthia was pleasurable; on the other hand, Kornfein worried whether he would succeed physically with this fabulous, but moody, beauty. He feared a gresile; he feared a fortzele. It seemed the act, somehow, stimulated Yiddish expressions in his mind, or, somehow, the sight of her caused it (he knew that she, like him, spoke the language). He noticed her pupikel, her nezlile, her tsitskes.

And what did she notice of his? He thought of Zeus's mistress Semele, just before she was burned to a crisp by a bolt of lightning hurled by Zeus for seeing her divine lover as he really was. Kornfein concentrated on carrying out the physical pursuits at hand, murmuring to her almost without being aware of it a series of endearments: my ketzele, my oystere, my kroynele. They ceased abruptly not because of what Kornfein perceived as Cynthia's mocking half smile or the martyred line of her brows, or even her displeased murmured "Oy" at the first endearment, "Oy vey" at the second, and "Oy vey is mir" at the last, but because of her telling him that he was a maskenspieler (a player of parts). Kornfein sighed, reflecting: why were even his most intimate moments invariably accompanied by a flavoring of vile farce.

Perhaps this feeling was connected to another one that Kornfein often had — that he was not living his life so much as narrating it. The curse, no doubt, of the writer.

And after Kornfein had "worked" and had more or less acquitted himself in his love-making with Cynthia and, having wiped the sweat off his forehead, exhausted like a hon nokh tashmish (a rooster after the hens have been serviced) yet immersed in the euphoria of successful release, his floating stage of post-coital bliss disturbed by Cynthia's chattering away — unlike Kornfein's ex-wife who promptly (and now, thought Kornfein, mercifully) slept following the act, Cynthia seemed to be stimulated to speech and was going on, a sound like the buzzing of bees in his ears.

Kornfein considered interrupting Cynthia's monologue; however, Cynthia was prattling on with such determination and rapidity that he thought it best not to interrupt her; she was going on about a painting in a gallery, or was it the gallery's owner, and then something about art and artists, quoting Modigliani that artists had different rights, different values than do normal, ordinary people because we (here she included herself among the artists) had different needs which put us above their standards, and the thought popped into Kornfein's mind that he wished he possessed at that moment a silken cord with which, like an Indian member of the murderous thugee cult, he would silence her. "You have an exquisite neck", he exclaimed suddenly to Cynthia. Actually, she possessed an elongated neck, longer than he preferred in women.

Cynthia reacted to his compliment to her neck by staring at him uncomprehendingly with her basalt black eyes. "You're not listening to a word I said," she said. Kornfein had learned that a 'conversation' with Cynthia could be an onerous proposition. It was hard to be a passive conversant with her — to listen, as was his wont.

Cynthia prodded, asked questions: "You understand?" "What do you say to that?" and so forth. You had to pay attention. A physically wearying process. When it was over, Kornfein felt as if had just finished a wrestling match or a five-set tennis contest. "Are you listening, Kornfein?" she would say if his attention flagged. If more exasperated, "Are you alive, Kornfein?" "Barely," he would whisper to himself. How had Levenstein put up with it? For his sin of "not listening" on the present occasion, he immediately apologized. "Oh, don't apologize," she admonished him, "I can't stand men who say 'I'm sorry.' (That's probably why she liked Levenstein, he thought). Just shut up." Nevertheless, he kissed her cheek and, resisting the urge to borrow the endearment "fire of my loins" from Humbert of 'Lolita', opted for murmuring a Yiddish tribute to her love-making, perhaps oy haat, zi mich anga banteshet. (Looking back later, he sometimes believed that their mutual affection for the Yiddish language prolonged their romantic relationship. But then he realized, with a pang, that it was her need for him to complete Levenstein's book which was the principal cause.) Mollified, (or, once again, it could be the fact that she remembered that she needed him for the book), Cynthia pulled a sheet over her nakedness and, with uncharacteristic generosity, was going to include him under the sheet with her, but he signaled her to wait.

Putting on his pajamas which lay sessile next to the bed, he then pulled the blanket over himself. Cynthia shook her head from side to side slowly, "I like to sleep

in the nude — you are a prude." In delivering this opinion, she rose to a sitting position, causing the sheet to
fall down and gather itself around her impressive thighs
(on one of which she was blessed with a plexus of small
veins shaped like a pink many-tentacled jelly fish con-
cerning which Kornfein made a mental note to kiss in
the future, perhaps accompanied by something verbally
appropriate, "jelly fish" presumably insufficiently lauda-
tory in Cynthia's nibbly ear). Thus appareled, Cynthia
reminded Kornfein of nothing so much as 'Victory',
the tricolor enveloping her thighs, mounting the barri-
cade. He decided against mentioning this praiseworthy
woman to Cynthia in his pique at her his being a prude
remark and simply explained to her that he cannot sleep
without pajamas. And, moreover, that the pajama collar
must be folded down, that he cannot sleep if the collar is
rubbing against his neck. "My neck is very sensitive," he
explained. (Would this make it easier for a thugee who
tried his silken cord on it? flashed through his mind, or
even for Cynthia with her long tapering fingers so soft
and yet powerful as a strangler's, as he recalled from that
first kiss of hers, when she took his face in her hands and
he felt like it was held in a vice.) "And the sleeves of my
pajama top I pull until they reach where the wrists join the
hands. I do not suffer the sleeves to move upward on my
arms, which causes me to feel exposed." (Here Cynthia
bestowed on him a look mixed of scorn and amusement,
or perhaps bemusement. He was not deterred.) He
explained that he carried out a parallel extending process

with his pajama pants — they have to reach his ankles. "The pillow," he added, "must be crisp and cool under my head." "Maybe you should substitute a lettuce," Cynthia observed, already half asleep, her custom to sleep naked obviating any necessity for such obsessive sleep-preluding ministrations. "Didn't Levenstein have any sleeping peccadilloes?" asked Kornfein hopefully. "He was too great a man for such foolishness," she snapped.

2

And so they became a twosome, Kornfein and Levenstein's wife, if a discreet twosome. And though neither was married and so did not need discretion, as if by unspoken arrangement, they maintained it. Actually, a discreet threesome — for Levenstein's book seemed - to Kornfein, at least - the third member of a melange-a-trois. It had a veritable presence. If Kornfein believed in spirits inhabiting objects, he might believe Levenstein had entered the book — a dybbuk to keep an eye on him. Perhaps for this reason, he took the precaution of ensuring that the manuscript lay within its paper bag when he made love to Cynthia.

Invariably, when he entered into bed she was still in the bathroom. It always took her a lot of time to take off her makeup, clean her face, spread all kinds of creams and check every millimeter of her face in the mirror to verify that no defect threatened her perfect skin. "Snow White's Mother Before the Glass", Kornfein dubbed such sessions

— to himself. How had the hardly patient Levenstein put up with it? Sandra had behaved in the opposite fashion — spurning makeup, she threw water on her face without creams and that was it. Maybe she considered her Junoesque figure and adequate features sufficient. Or perhaps she hadn't even thought about it at all, but acted, as in so many other ways, with a naturalness that became her. It was that naturalness that Kornfein remembered with a pang when Cynthia's artifice rankled him. If so, why did he feel so passionate about Cynthia, something he had felt, if at all, only at the beginning of his and Sandra's relationship. Certainly, it was more than a case of opposites attract. He regretted never having asked Levenstein what had attracted him to Cynthia. But, of course, he would never have dared to ask such a question.

Kornfein sometimes looked in the same mirror to make sure his eyebrows pre-coitus were smoothed down (more a habit than a beauty-aid, or perhaps a superstition); he refrained from doing so if Cynthia was present lest she consider it effeminate. When he gazed at himself in the mirror, there occasionally came to him Joseph Chaim Brenner's observation: 'If a writer looks in the mirror at the hour of his writing he will see the face of a murderer.' Kornfein once asked Levenstein if he understood what Brenner meant. "He probably meant that writing for the true writer was a matter of life or death. Or maybe he was thinking of the writer-critic under full steam," he added, pleased with the self-irony implicit in his second interpretation.

Lovers are rarely equally matched. Certainly not the couple before us. Her physical baggage gave her the edge; also, her dominating personality. And Kornfein did not always concentrate on the matter at hand, plagued by what he dubbed his "philosophical athleticism"; a result of his natural talent for literary serendipity whereby he chanced upon interesting and valuable things, supplemented by a compulsion to make such things known. What was it about himself, Kornfein had wondered, that caused him not to be able to enjoy even sex without literary associations bedeviling him? Sighing, he knew the answer: it was the price of being a writer. Cynthia probably treated his sigh as a manifestation of sexual satisfaction; better not to disabuse her.

And he recalled the instance when he was dutifully trying to please Cynthia, snug against the harp strings of her ribs, so to speak — an image that had just come to him (from somewhere) and with regard to which he was deliberating on whether to transfer to his tongue and proffer to the owner of — when she suddenly sat up in bed and, to his amazement, sang the first seven notes of the major scale, doh, re, mi, fa, so, la, ti... and stopped. "You feel the aching incompleteness that so wants satisfaction of a final 'doh', Kornfein? That's what I feel with you in bed. Your mind has shifted elsewhere — surely captured by a literary thought. A musical one, but no matter."

Once, naked, she insisted on playing the harp for him, as a prelude to their lovemaking. A nice blending of the baroque and the bawdy. As she stood next to her harp before doing so, her hand on his shoulder, there flashed in his mind the painting 'Kreutzer Sonata' in which the violinist lover kisses Pozonyshev's wife as she stands near the piano. Kornfein surmised that Cynthia's downing a couple of drinks before he arrived was responsible for her good spirits. With whom had she been drinking? he couldn't help wondering. He knew better than to ask. The Latin motto Nemo me impune lacessit: "No one provokes me with impunity" seemed tailor-made for her. Kornfein had once mused that it should be inscribed on Levenstein's gravestone, but now decided that it applied no less to Cynthia. Thus non-attired (Kornfein was embarrassed but feigned not, remaining in his underpants to the last minute despite her cajoling to join her in her state of nature), she played for him "Drink to Me Only with Thine Eyes", which she knew he liked, but only played for him when she was in a good mood, otherwise turning up her nose at it as "too saccharine," a category in which she included his other favorite, "The Last Rose of Summer." (She once chided him that he didn't know the difference between Bach and Offenbach. He replied, truthfully, "I like Offenbach.") She favored more "demanding" pieces, such as 'La Fille aux Cheveux de Lin' and Debussy's "Sonata in C minor." Cynthia believed (or perhaps feigned belief in) the supremacy of "artistic composers" as opposed to "popular composers". "Pure" music, as she denominated it, and not incidental music: compositions for ballet, or the theater, or (worst of all) the movies, or even light classical music (which Kornfein favored). When he retorted that Stravinsky's 'The Rite of Spring' had brought about a revolution in composition despite being music written for the dance, Cynthia glowered at him a long moment before dissembling, "There are better rites of spring than dancing."

In fidelity to the rite, Kornfein took her — he had finally removed his underpants; she had then removed her last item of wear: red bikini underpants, and there flashed in his mind Lolita in her Aztec Red bathing briefs. Apparently his "taking her" hadn't been forceful enough, or perhaps she was back on their conflicting musical tastes, because she suddenly exclaimed, "I am a person of arias. You, Kornfein, are a person of recitatives." And she added, "You deserve to make love to the 'Minute Waltz.'" "Ok, ok," he tried to calm her, "I got carried away..." and there came to him, as if in Levenstein's voice, the Yiddish coda: "Man digs his grave with his sex organ." She was about to make a cutting reply — leydekgeyer"(good for nothing), but apparently suddenly remembered the purpose of it all — the book. She hugged him. "It's ok, Korn, nisht gefeldelt." Kornfein was delighted by the "Korn"; it was the first time she had used the affectionate nom d'amour, eminently preferable to the more distancing, "Kornfein." He did not know it then, but it was the last time she called him "Korn." He had wanted to ask her if she called Levenstein "Lev" similarly, yet he feared to ask her. He remembered that in the beginning of their relationship he had called her affectionately "Cyn." "Cynthia," she corrected. "My name is 'Cynthia.'" Maybe "Cyn" sounded too much like "Sin."

With time and on most occasions, Kornfein and Cynthia managed sufficiently for each other's pleasure — or feigned pleasure, he could never be sure with her. But it didn't matter, Cynthia belonged to him. Although once, again falling into his recidivist literary mode (did sexual relations stimulate it, or was the reverse true?), he could not resist a reference while in medius res to the words from a story of the Israeli writer, S. Yizhar's: "gripping the horse's silky mane and its warm churning muscles" and she had pushed him off her in anger, muttering in Yiddish, in d'rerd arayn, quite forcefully by dint of her muscular arms, the result of her harp playing over the years (an unfeminine aspect he did not care for, preferring suppleness in women), which led him to speculate whether the literary intrusions were subconsciously more precious to him than her sounds of satisfaction or of feigned pleasure.

Once, as he was lying on the sofa in the salon, reading a book he had chosen from a bookshelf — "Anatomy of Criticism", a quondam 'classic' on criticism by Northrop Frye), Cynthia, in a mood of romantic high spirits, playfully opened the zipper on his pants. Kornfein, not in the mood for the more practical anatomy which Cynthia evidently had in mind, tried to dissuade her, prompting her to accuse him of "lacking spontaneity" and of "thinking everything out". Then she cursed him or perhaps it was intended as advice: "ez zol dir dunern in boykh un blitzin in di hoyzn" (You should have thunder in your belly and lightning in your pants).

3

Plato said that in order to know itself, a soul must observe another soul. And so I observed Cynthia, verily. But if the other soul lacks a soul, then what? Yet I am being over-dramatic, a trait I may have absorbed via osmosis from Cynthia. When I say she lacked a soul, I mean with regard to myself; as for others... there were times I doubted Cynthia's devotion to me.

As, for instance, that day as I came to visit her — unannounced (she had in the beginning of our relationship insisted that I telephone her or she me to fix my visits to her, pleading "harp rehearsals and performance scheduling"), having chanced to secure two tickets to a highly acclaimed play for a performance that very evening and wanting to surprise Cynthia and take her to the play. As I climbed the stairs to her apartment, I heard from behind a door, a recording of the furious violin of the first movement of Beethoven's 'Kreutzer Sonata'; thereafter I passed a man descending the stairs who looked familiar. In profile, he looked like a Roman emperor. His black hair was swept back behind large ears, showing a high forehead and a forceful, prominent nose. The eyebrows, arched more on the right than on the left, indicated a mixture of wisdom and humor, or perhaps irony; clear blue eyes under heavy eyelids reflected a certain old-world vanity and charm. He was a well-known gallery owner-cum-painter, Bernard Krim by name.

Krim was, like his near-named, Benya Krik, the Jewish gangster "King" of Issac Babel's Odessa stories, a fabulous dresser. If Krik preferred an orange suit and a diamond bracelet, Krim went in for the dark striped suits of a Mafioso don, often garnished with a red rose in the lapel and, somewhat incongruously, contrasted by bedazzling brightly colored shirts with the initials of his name emblazoning the pocket. The shirts specifically designed for him (according to his claim) or (according to rumor), the initials skillfully sewn on by a paramour-painter in return for exhibiting her paintings free of charge in his gallery.

This description may be tendentious on my part (though Levenstein called him "the Jewish Narcissus"); since I was an indifferent dresser, although I strove to improve the situation to please Cynthia, alas failing to satisfy her in this department. "Itzik Manger," she called me. If at first her comparing me to the great Yiddish poet pleased me (while mystifying me as I didn't write poetry), I soon came to realize that she was mocking my sartorial efforts. Manger, I learned, favored a disheveled appearance — even to walking around with a rope holding up his pants.

To get back to Krim, he was a brash, garrulous man who took far more words than necessary to tell more than he knew (pooh-poohed by Levenstein as his "torrential eloquence"). Krim sported a closed-cropped beard, of the type that is called in Yiddish a berdelle. (There are also the lengthy, dignified beard, the bord, the medium-length beard, the berdel, and various other beards: the berdinke, the berdinkelle, the berdinyunkele, and the berdinyuntshekel. Such information is not essential to our narrative, but like the facts about whales amassed in "Moby Dick," may add to it.)

I could not be sure that Krim had just come from visiting Cynthia, as her apartment was one floor above where we passed each other, yet the suspicion that he had gnawed at me. One not lessened by the aroma of liquor which followed in his wake, or did I imagine this? My suspicion was confirmed when I knocked on her door and Cynthia opened it and a surprised expression formed on her face before she managed to cover it. Cynthia had apparently expected the knocker to be the gallery owner come back to tell her something he had forgotten to say to her. Her obsidian eyes widened in anger. She stood, hands on hips in her angry fishwife pose, familiar to me from other displays of displeasure. "What are you doing here?" she asked in a frigid tone. "Didn't I tell you to always phone first."

Cynthia was sensitive on the subject of phoning. A late riser, unless "artistic commitments" — her words for harp appearances — didn't allow it, she refused to speak on the phone before two in the afternoon. Levenstein had been an earlier riser. I suspected that in the present instance, it being evening, her reminding me of her demand to phone first derived from more sinister motives. Somebody's query buffeted me: "Will love come after the betrayal or before?"

I felt as if my heart was being crushed by a giant fist — an image I immediately recognized as the sentiments of the protagonist of I.B. Singer's 'The Magician of Lublin.' Despite my very real angst, I pictured Levenstein shaking his head, if not his fist, at my having borrowed the bathetic image; at the same time, he would appreciate my not living my life sans literary annotation.

My good intentions (alas, the very things 'the way to hell is paved with') in coming to Cynthia were now packed in permafrost. I tried to rescue the situation. "Not two hours ago I received two tickets to the current play hit 'Media'. I wanted to surprise you."

There ensued a silence, brief but of seeming endless duration, during which the orange curtains seemed to rustle in empathic impatience. There was a certain tension in the air. With Cynthia there was always a certain tension in the air — even in moments of (relative) tranquility. Not for the first time, I wondered how she and Levenstein had managed with each other. After what appeared to be a struggle to maintain her equipoise, Cynthia deigned to speak.

"You surprised me," she said in a kind of mumbled growl, dabbing a handkerchief scented with her perfume at the area of her decolletage, a nervous gesture on her part which caused me to suddenly recall the description by the wife of Isaac Babel of how, when a Soviet secret policeman came to collect trousers, socks and handkerchiefs for her imprisoned husband, she scented the handkerchiefs heavily with her own perfume. She explained, "I so much wanted to send Babel a greeting from home, even if it was just a familiar scent." I was jolted from this recollection — and from a discomfort caused by her then dabbing her lips with her perfumed handkerchief, perhaps in an effort to cover the odor of sherry or whatever — by Cynthia raising her voice to a full shout," I don't like surprises, I like things arranged."

To my chagrin, I noted that she stood in the doorway and did not invite me in. On the table I spied a giant cornucopia of flowers whose horn shape seemed to mock me with its decidedly masculine aspect. It seemed the gift of a dandy, a fop, a poseur, a petite-maître, as the French put it (Krim was shorter than Cynthia). Attached to the cornucopia was a card on which was written: "Grand passions are as rare as masterpieces" It smacked of Krim, alright.

"So… you're not free to come with me?" I persisted gamely.

She seemed to think this over. I had the feeling that she was weighing the uncompleted novel of Levenstein, her late husband, that I had agreed to complete against — who knows what? I prepared myself for her propensity, especially when impatient or displeased, to answering my questions with a curt "Yes" or "No."

"Why not?" she said, in a voice of what seemed to me forced gaiety.

Cynthia took a step toward me, and then stopped

suddenly, to allow herself a final look in the mirror. "Varicose veins, puffy ankles, saggy breasts," she said under her breath. I had never noticed any of these defects, but then Cynthia was a cosmetic hypochondriac. Suppressing a chuckle upon remembering Levenstein's amused comment that only an Englishman could regard women as "inefficient organisms because they have too many protuberances," I avoided looking at her protu-berances, on the one hand (including her "Rubenesque derriere," as Krim once described it to Cynthia) and her shoes, on the other, lest, with regard to the latter, she perceive I had spotted something amiss and begin to rethink her choice.

Behind her, I noticed on the corner of the dressing-table the little mother-of-pearl inlaid frame containing a photograph taken by a sidewalk photographer. Cynthia looked radiant, Levenstein tired or distracted. Maybe the shorter Levenstein found it difficult to match her long-legged stride. In truth, in all the years we worked together, Levenstein never took me into his confidence about his relationship with his wife. He may have hinted at it after I told him that Sandra and I were going to be divorced. "I read about a lecture in Yiddish in pre-war Poland whose title was 'Man and Wife: The Problem of Problems.'"

Why did Cynthia agree to accompany me to the theater? Perhaps because a theater afforded her an audience; Cynthia would be seen. For her, the external world existed to revolve exclusively around her person.

She epitomized the concept that one's true self is that which exists in the gaze of others. If my relief that she had agreed to come with me was dampened by these thoughts, during the play other thoughts disturbed me more. The picture of the gallery owner descending the stairs repeated itself over and over in my mind like, if I recalled rightly, the murderer descending the stairs in the movie, Spiral Staircase. I refrained from trying to besmirch Krim's character: it might backfire.

True, Levenstein didn't exactly fit the dramatic mode, but he was a 'dominant' type which she could sympathize with. I, of course, had no place in this company, being neither dramatic nor physically dominant. Thick in the shoulders and legs, Krim suited Levenstein's description that he "would make a good support for an acrobatic troupe's pyramid." ("Thickset," I once described his build; Cynthia's frown prevented further exegesis.) A quality which came in handy when, at a cocktail party or paintings exhibition, he spied a beautiful woman (Levenstein maintained that Krim had a prejudice against women who were not beautiful) talking to a man. He would plant his mass in front of the latter, blocking him out of the conversation, and begin subjecting the woman to his verbal charm, abetted by a deep baritone voice. Levenstein claimed the voice accounted for ninety percent of his charm with the opposite sex. I claimed it was his eyes, grey-blue in color that seemed to look through you, capable of causing in some women a certain libidinal frisson. Also good for staring down rivals. Cynthia attributed his attractiveness to women to his nose "strong and eagle-beaked as a Medici's" (no less). More than once over the years a question gnawed at me: Did Levenstein have suspicions about Krim and Cynthia? Try as I could, I couldn't remember a clue.

Krim had an eye for ample pulchritude, for zaftig declivity and rise. Cynthia fit the bill.

The questionable character of Krim — a fact which I had not raised with Cynthia lest she start accusing of 'guilt by association' — was the result of a minor scandal some years back in which (I recalled) he had been involved, something about selling copied works of art as originals. ("Jason in pursuit of the golden fleece," as Levenstein succinctly put it, for all of his lack of empathy for Greek mythology. He also bestowed on Krim the sobriquet "King Schmear" — presumably a play on words on King Lear). Monet said motifs require seeking, but Krim didn't trouble to look too far. It was said of Krim that he had imitated so many still lives in the seventeenth century style that the sheen of the pewter plates, the glint on the empty wineglasses and the flash of light on the long neck of the porcelain pitcher were second nature to him. Sometimes he applied the same technique to nineteenth and twenti-eth century styles to produce modern still lifes "lost but fortuitously discovered" of ________ and ______, adding patriotic American motifs, when necessary, to literally complete the picture. As for example in his 'improving' Magritte's 'The Great Table' — fortunately for Krim, his clients weren't art connoisseurs. He retitled it "Oranges at the Beach". The original had portrayed a bowl of apples, the total in blue against a sky blue and clouded and with a scimitar moon, sand and sea in the background. Krim substituted oranges and added a lifeguard stand and two beach volley-ball players. He eliminated the crescent moon, perhaps he considered it too politically charged.

Bouncing back from the forgeries contretemps (his guiding principle seemingly that of the Russian impresario Sergei Diaghilev: "Success is the only thing that redeems everything and covers up everything"), Krim had become successful as a seller of copied works of art as copies. "My copies are better than the originals," he boasted. "They are charged with a numinous inner life which the originals fail to display." Another attribution to him: "If the forgeries were moved from the museums, their walls would be half empty."

It was an indication of our times that forgeries were acquired because they were forgeries. Things had almost reached the absurd reflected in Woodie Allen's claim that his apartment was hung with Picassos done by Van Gogh. Krim, if not quite capable of approaching the latter feat, might very well pull off a claim that he had a painting of Van Gogh by Picasso. Picasso Krim. Apropos of Picasso (and Krim), Levenstein said re Krim's proclivity for repetition, "Picasso painted 49 bulls, but Krim's not Picasso."

Krim chose to wrap his creative self-deceit in a smokescreen of rants against his critics ("The artist's body radiates light from every wound"), self-aggrandizement, and even a self-suggested comparison with Raphael (Cynthia bristled when I pointed out that Raphael died allegedly of amorous excess) — whereas, in practice, his art fell within the conceptual framework of Thomas Mann's 'The Confessions of Felix Krull, Confidence Man.' Krim had gotten so good at playing 'Krim' that it was difficult to say whether he was acting or not.

Krim's personal taste in art, I suspected, ran to paintings such as 'The Sultan's Favorite Returning from the Bath.' Schmaltz synergized to sex. He without doubt would claim he was faithful to Picasso's dictum, when asked about the difference between art and eroticism, "But there is no difference." (Levenstein once observed that "Krim uses art to inflame the passions — of his would-be conquests; Plato knew what he was doing when he banned artists from his Republic.") Yet it was another painting — Arshile Gorky's 'Diary of a Seducer' that I invariably associated with Krim, because of its title; I doubted that Krim fancied the abstract expressionist painting, if indeed he was aware of its existence.

I refrained from verbally assailing Krim's taste in Cynthia's hearing (the felicitous description "art brut" hovered on my lips, as well as a recalled less blunt characterization by Levenstein, "pretensions to connoisseurship") lest she reply (not for the first time), "You have no taste, Kornfein. Worse, you are a master of bad taste." This was a variation of one of Levenstein's favorite critical bashing phrases, "________ not so much lacks taste as is a master of bad taste." And Krim had good taste? The same Krim who, as Levenstein once enlightened me as a result Cynthia's dragging him from time to time to galleries (including Krim's baroque/art deco decor "studio") "where she liked to be the center of attention of the fine-shemekers" (hoity-toity). He was fond of delivering the same cigar waving monologue about Rembrandt's subtle blendings of light and shadow, of Reubens' sweeping lines and sensuous portrayals of flesh and fabrics, of Renoir's soft tones, of Van Gogh's brilliant colors, "all of which techniques," Levenstein added, "Krim had learned to copy onto his canvases, according to need. And even his prepared megillah sounds copied. Kim affects the elegant, imperturbable Olympian displaying his aplomb — if under the patina there lurks a Yiddish chutzpa."

Cynthia liked to refer to Krim as "my cher maître" — perhaps to needle me. I wondered if Cynthia had referred to Krim as her "cher maître" in Levenstein's day as she did in mine. The title conjured up an Old Master painter in smock and beret; Krim was too fashion-conscious for such unprepossessing garb—he would opt for an Edwardian smoking jacket, overly garnished with some Krimian touch. Levenstein once quipped that the only prop Krim lacked was Salvatore Dali's perfume-disseminating cane. In order to get back at her for using this nominis umbra, I would refer to him as her petit-maitre, meaning a dandy, a fop, but also an artist of minor importance. She applied to it its literal meaning of 'little master', unaware of its pejorative usage. Once I realized this, I ceased to use the title.

On one occasion, I forbore not and mocked his latest gimmick of putting a bit of actual sand in his paintings of the desert, or coral in his beach epics.

"Authenticity!" thundered Cynthia. "Trompe l'oeil."

"Trompe la poche," I countered.

On a second occasion, I said about Krim, "Every single sentence of his oozes artifice and pose."

"He is wonderfully theatrical," she countered. "His nostrils stretch, flare, go through all sorts of flourishes that bend every vowel and consonant."

I switched from ad hominem attack to assailing his brush. "Not to speak of his paintings which exemplify Warhol's statement that art is 'what you can get away with.'"

Cynthia raised an eyebrow; actually, both eyebrows; she did nothing by halves. "You're jealous of him because he knows more about paintings than you do."

"Never, never, never, never, never," I exclaimed, borrowing from King Lear.

"Don't exaggerate, Kornfein. Going to a gallery with Krim is like seeing with four eyes, my two and his two."

To this visual simile I responded, under my breath, with a fulgurant Yiddish curse directed at the all-seeing Krim: "Aroy sknikhn zoln dir di oygn fun kop" (May your eyes crawl out of your head), which may sound harsh falling on the ears of the non-Yiddish reader but is comparatively mild as Yiddish curses go. I, alas, lacked the killer instinct of the late Levenstein and Cynthia (one of the few apparent bonds between them), and so settled for (the admittedly more mundane) statement to Cynthia that in my opinion Krim was a failure as a painter and a person. Cynthia jumped to his defense. "Your problem is that you feel yourself consistently under-appreciated."

"Me!"

"You!"

So much for pronoun discourse. And after Cynthia had thus raised her cudgels against me, she now took them up to defend Krim by quoting the poor besmirched (drawing herself up in her Aida pose and with a voice to match), "In our life there is a single color, as on an artist's palette, which provides the meaning of life and art. It is the color of love." Unfortunately, its source didn't come to me until two days later (found in a book of quotations under "Love") — Marc Chagall. When I pointed it out to Cynthia, she replied, "Are you still going on about Krim?" Vanquished, but at least she called him "Krim" and not "my cher maitre." When I threw out my final word on the subject, hinting at Krim's dalliances, Cynthia replied that he was a "homme à femmes." She made it sound like a compliment. I wanted to put her homme à femmes hors d'usage, but I was ill equipped to compete with his repertoire of hand-kissing, bowing, fussing over, flowers, and raised-glass toasting. The antithesis of myself — and (food for thought here) Levenstein. I settled for mumbling, "'homme d'affairs' — romantic affairs."

"Why do you always focus on peccadillos?"

"Peccadillos!"

"Trifles."

Silence.

"You're a prude. P-R-U-D-E."

"Thanks for spelling it out."

"At least Krim is never sullen."

This I took as a dig at yours truly. The word she had used disturbed me. 'Moody', 'glum', 'sulky', even 'morose', I could live with. Not 'sullen'..

"Enough of quibbling, Kornfein. I have to practice my harp now."

I took my leave.

On a later occasion, Cynthia hinted that she was experiencing a "down" period with Krim, apparently stemming from her refusal to play a harp version of 'Pictures at an Exhibition' as background to an exhibition of his paintings, with an explanation that "there is no harp arrangement for the music." Failing that, Krim wanted her to use her influence with the conductor of our city's philharmonic, to arrange for some of his charges (Krim's word) to play Ravel's arrangement of the music or, at worst, to supply a pianist to play Mussorgsky's original version for piano. She declined these options, with some excuse that left Krim miffed. I seized on the opportunity of this saga and, more importantly, her subsequent disparagement of Krim, to toss off a disparaging remark of my own about Krim after she ignored my subtler barb that the 'Kreutzer Sonata' might have been a more appropriate musical accompaniment (perhaps its significance vis-à-vis Krim and the lover in Tolstoy's book of the same name went over her head).

Cynthia shook her head in her hair-fluffing gesture of dismissal of my criticism of Krim, "He is, when not in his debonair, courtly mood, an oppressive man, insufferable, unpleasant to be with. But he is an artist. You don't understand, Kornfein, the art world stresses the cult of the personality." I couldn't help thinking that this might explain her attraction to Levenstein! At the same time, I felt insulted — that I didn't measure up in her eyes, lacking in sufficient caliber. Apropos of nothing (or maybe something) Cynthia added, "He has wonderfully sensual full lips." Nu, I thought, unconsciously fingering my own, unremarkable lips, neither full nor thin. Cynthia's reluctance to break off with Krim was consistent with her ability, when necessary, to slam a door without quite closing it. And Krim was second to no one in his ability to get a foot in the door.

As much as I disliked Krim (I had ever since someone — who? Cynthia in a bitchy mood, Levenstein in a malicious one, told me that Krim dismissed me as "Levenstein's Boswell"), at times when I contemplated some of Krim's oeuvre, I felt a degree of awe — a sensation not identical with aesthetic pleasure. Awe at the ambition — at the pulling it off. For all of Krim's foolhardy bravado, there was a touching fearlessness about his artistic life which I would not admit to Cynthia, and only rarely to myself (embodied or rationalized in Krim's pronouncement, "When you come right down to it, all you have is yourself."). This aspect of Krim caused me to think of Picasso's 'Buste' — a portrait of a mustachioed bravo topped with a fanciful green hat and caparisoned in a black patterned red cloak and white ruff. Surely Krim (knowledgeable about paintings, whatever his artifice, a knowledge that Levenstein had dismissed, unfairly in my opinion, as "low-style connoisseurship", adding, in a pithy, if uncharacteristic, blend of the French and the Yiddish, "a petit maven") was aware of it also.

But the gallery owner/forgeries maven may have had company. This should not have surprised me. Cynthia was singularly accessible to all demonstrations of regard. One day I happened to be downtown and spied a man talking to Cynthia. I couldn't hear him from where I stood; with his emphatic gestures, he seemed a shadow boxer. I recognized him as a macher in the garment workers organization. He stared at her like a cat at milk. Suddenly he leaned closer to her ear and whispered something, while placing a hand on her shoulder, most familiarly. Whatever he had enlightened her with seemed to cause her eyes to sparkle, as they did when she talked of music or art, or when she listened to an especially juicy bit of gossip. My potential rival: none other than Barry Kahn, the would be-gantze knaker, whom Cynthia had once mentioned to me. Perhaps in keeping with our increasingly capitalistic times, he wore a tie. It was, at least, socialist red, yet its color in my eyes, seemed more phallic than political, and it reminded me of the red tie worn by Aschenbach at the end of 'Death in Venice.' Then, oddly, the words of the socialist hymn flashed through my mind: 'Awake for the day is coming.' They were clearly a warning.

But what disturbed me most about this meeting was Cynthia's attire. She wore an ankle-length evening dress of red, gold, and black, tight-fitted to her body, not covering the slight bulge of her body, which once, catching me noting it, she defended as her "Mound of Venus", Nu, and the dress revealed a goodly portion of her back. My ex, Sandra, would surely have commented, "The only thing missing is an imitation gold cigarette holder." 'Holly Dolly' was my own contribution. Cynthia had never dressed up like that for me. But what disturbed me, oddly enough, was Cynthia's red shoes. She had never donned red shoes for me, and the thought that she wore them for this rendezvous — if it was that and not a chance meeting — gnawed at me. And as if the red shoes and evening dress were not enough, as they walked together, Cynthia leaned on his arm. She had never walked like that in public with me.

I tried to discern if anything in her glances toward him offered him promises of assignations to come. Her I wanted to choke. Bakunin said, "The urge to destroy is also a creative urge." I didn't feel particularly creative at the moment. I hurried away lest Cynthia discover me, trying to salvage something of my honor by drawing a parallel between my situation and Proust's spying on Albertine!

As you can well imagine, this possible proliferation of competitors has a bad effect on me. My distress was but a little mollified when one night in her sleep Cynthia mumbled, "Not a single one of them deserved me." Surely, she meant men, but whether the two suitors or all men, I could not know, nor would I dare to inquire.

Two weeks later, visiting Cynthia, I was sipping tea and she sherry. Between swallows, Cynthia was yawning prodigiously, a not surprising prelude to her comment on how fatigued she was, which I took as a clear signal that there would be no physical rapport between us that evening, and in the midst of one of these yawns (I thought of the saying, "I talk with you and sleep with him"), the phone rang.

Cynthia pounced on it, suddenly most awake, and began speaking in a low voice. I thought I caught the scornful words "der forsher" (the investigator) — presumably a not-so-veiled reference to myself as suspicious of her. "Di zomlerkeh" (the collector) I mentally retorted, with her "collecting" of suitors in mind. The conversation was of brief duration. I thought I caught the words, "Not now," before she ended it.

Her last words poured cold water on any hopes on my part that his call represented the 'Final Soliloquy of the Interior Paramour,' to borrow from Wallace Stevens. I felt like one of Arthur Schnitzler's Viennese cuckolds, if technically not a cuckold since Cynthia was not my wife. My critic's awareness then led me to abandon Viennese cuckolds to identify with more contemporary literary cuckolds, Bellow's Herzog, and that most wonderful example of the genre, Cynthia Ozick's Edelshtein.

Unmindful of my anguish, Cynthia seated herself primly on the sofa, smiled at me, and took a healthy swig from her sherry. "You don't mind of it's a short visit, tonight, do you?" Her she yawned vociferously as if Rip Van Winkle himself had just woken up after decade of sleep. I nodded my agreement. A Yiddish expression entered my head, offering little comfort: az a nar halt di ku bay di herner, ken zi a kluger melk'n. (When a fool holds a cow by the horns, a wise man can milk her.) All of this, of course, did not help my work on the unfinished book of her late husband Levenstein that Cynthia insisted I complete.

<h1 style="text-align:center">4</h1>

Kornfein continued to visit Cynthia, and she to receive him, despite their mutual, if ne'er expressed, knowledge that their relationship wasn't completely based on love; Kornfein knew, perhaps had always known, that Levenstein's book was the real glue that held the one to the other. Agnon wrote: "Anyone who has to do with women knows that a love which depends upon the physical bond alone will come to end before long." Kornfein opted to be in thrall to the sentiment expressed in the Yiddish: "Aby men zeht zikh." And before he went to her, as always, he inspected himself in the mirror to ensure that he would be at his physical best, remembering with a pang that until he instituted the practice with regard to Cynthia, he hadn't done so since his courtship of Sandra days.

Kornfein's recalling of his courtship of Sandra afforded a certain pleasure. Had not Sandra once remarked to him, "You live in a life of déjà vues"? And now she is one of them and part of them. Before meeting her, he hadn't been popular with girls (too nebech, he pronounced judgment). He had attributed his lack of popularity to being a poor dancer.

Cynthia was a talker; Kornfein a non-talker. It hadn't bothered Cynthia, she talked enough for both of them. His part of the deal (the unspoken deal, appropriately enough) was that he had to listen. To her. If she caught him not paying attention to one of her soliloquies, she let him know it in no uncertain terms. "Say something so I know you are still alive" or "Nu, you have a tongue?" Or she simply damned him "the inzikhist." ("the introspective.") Once when she employed one of these choice epithets, he replied laconically that the Gnostics said that every thought has already been thought before.

"Dreck," she replied.

"That, too," he countered.

"Not in Yiddish," she said.

In his opinion the most brilliant thing she ever said. (Levenstein would have loved her answer.)

Less brilliant, but also something which Kornfein didn't forget, was the coda. "Kornfein, you're the world champion of unimportant details."

"You mean literary ones?"

"No — life ones."

She sounded like Sandra.

If Levenstein's utterances (like his reviews) were strong, sharp, penetrating and employed irony with an intent to hurt, Cynthia matched him in the force of her utterances, when miffed at something or someone (usually Kornfein), though she resorted less to irony. (Kornfein suspected she lacked the patience for irony). She could be as coarse as a fish-monger and a look of hers could rob you of the power of speech (an attribute not overly-developed in him, anyhow). Yet sometimes she saw something remarkable in even the most matter-of-fact and banal things. It was then that Kornfein cherished her most. Yet if he occasionally manifested a similar approach, she criticized him. The lash of her tongue sometimes caused Kornfein to miss Sandra. Sandra and he were two of a kind. Neither too much talk, nor too little. An odd combination, Cynthia — lax at the mouth, disciplined at the harp. An odder combination with him: the galitzianer meets the yekhe. A good horror movie title, mused Kornfein, trying to make light of their differences.

More than once Kornfein tried to put his finger on exactly why he and Sandra had agreed on a divorce. Perhaps the prosaic answer was that their marriage had simply wound down like a tired old clock, or according to a kind of matrimonial law of entropy. (Once he overheard her say on the telephone to a friend the words "protracted tedium" in connection with living with him. Flaubert contended that writers should be orderly and predictable in their lives so they can be savage and sinister in their work. Kornfein defied this dictum. He was orderly and predictable in both spheres. Sometimes he felt uncomfortable about his "Henry James syndrome." He winced at remembering Cynthia's saying to him, "Every life has its top side and its reverse side. (pause) Not yours of course, Kornfein.")

Or perhaps the end of their marriage was a reflection of its beginning. He had one day simply asked Sandra to marry him, out of the blue, since the proposal had not come at a restaurant, or together with the offering of a ring, but as they were sitting on a bench in a park during a lengthy pause in conversation. One minute Kornfein was watching the pigeons peck at food, the next he had popped the question. Whenever he thought of this prosaic event, Kornfein identified with the poet W. H. Auden who said that on a rare date with a girl, "I couldn't think of anything to say, so I asked her to marry me." And, like Auden, Kornfein, on dates, found it hard to keep the conversation going. He had even considered leaving a copy of Justine — a book he was smitten by at the time — in various places with the hope that a young woman would find it, read it, contact him (his name and phone number would be written in the book) and by this means he would not only find his 'soul mate', but would have something to talk about (Justine) when they met!

He never actually put the plan into operation.

Kornfein sometimes wondered if, like the Vicar of Wakefield, he hadn't chosen his wife for such qualities as would wear well. Or perhaps he chose her because of her high cheekbones suggesting the Tartar and the fantasies they aroused. If the latter, they turned out to be misleading. For her part, Sandra once confessed to him, though of dubious veracity since their marriage was then on the downswing, that she had married him for "his good heart and nice hand at word play." The first part of this confession a painful, if more gentle reminder, of Levenstein's ultimate insult in this vein — that Kornfein reminded him of the person in a Russian poem so enchanted by the purity of his soul that he catches himself kissing his own hands. What offense on his part had warranted such ill-treatment? He couldn't remember. Probably it lay long buried in his subconscious. To Sandra's credit, when early on he had told her of his writing hopes for the future, and his hesitation, she responded, "Your life is writing. So write." Even the divorce could not blight the memory of that moment.

On the other hand, she once said to him, "You have a hole in your soul that will never be filled," a phrase which repeated itself in his mind from time to time. On one occasion he quoted to Cynthia what Sandra had said about him. She pursed her lips without answering.

"Nu?" he prompted.

"Do you expect me to fill it?" she replied in a tone of

exasperation. It was his turn not to answer.

"I'm not a soul dentist," she added for good measure, not one for opening up with one barrel when she could open up with two. Sandra would get a kick out of her answer, he thought. Levenstein for sure. He himself failed to appreciate the humor of it. Maybe Cynthia wasn't a soul dentist, Kornfein reflected ruefully, but she had struck a nerve.

As had Sandra, when Kornfein overheard her say on the phone to a friend that her life had been ruined by literature. Or was she merely quoting a character in a book? Or was she identifying with the character in a book? He strained to hear in order to verify, hopefully, that Sandra was not connecting herself to the sentiment expressed. He abandoned the effort for fear she would catch him listening. He would not ask her outright.

And here he suddenly remembered that on the day of the divorce proceeding, as they waited for their turn, Sandra wore a blue skirt and an orange sweater, although she usually avoided contrasting colors. And he had smiled a wry smile, recalling that some writer — he couldn't remember who — in his novel had used throughout it the colors blue and orange. And even though he, Kornfein, was about to be divorced from Sandra, he thought about pointing it out to her, it being, after all, a 'friendly divorce', but they were then summoned to appear and he forgot about it — until now.

After the divorce, Levenstein comforted him, in his

way. "You find solace in sentences," he told him. Oddly, Sandra had once used the very words. Then, he had dissembled and said, "Only in your arms." She scowled, not one for hyperbole.

He no longer had Sandra and Cynthia was not his; maybe that's why he was putting so much hope into "Levenstein's" novel. And why he had told Cynthia that the book would be published as written by Levenstein and him.

"No, as written by Levenstein," she corrected.

Her words stunned him. "That's not fair," he stammered.

"Levenstein is Levenstein — the famous critic. I intend to preserve his reputation."

His reputation was built on my labor.

What is important is the persona. The persona was Levenstein. He is a literary presence. You, Kornfein, let us be honest, are not." You were assistant critic, not the critic. You will remain the "silent partner."

"And what am I to receive for this — contribution — on my part? To put it bluntly, what do I get out of it?"

She had been standing before him. Now she raised her long index finger and pointed to herself.

Kornfein was flabbergasted. Yet the gesture, she standing framed against her harp in the background, sacrificing herself for Levenstein, struck him to the core. He felt like The Beast receiving Beauty against her will. Yet he wanted her — permanently. Yeats' words came to him: "The uncontrollable mystery on the bestial floor."

He said nothing. He simply nodded. The master

of words wordless. Without a word, she led him to the bedroom. Without a word they undressed. To seal the deal, he supposed. Did he feel like a pimp? Kornfein did. At the same time, he was delighted. And he could not help thinking: Levenstein would get his book. But, contrary to what Kornfein had believed all his life, literature wasn't everything.

Once again, Cynthia made love like she played the harp, perfunctorily. Kornfein didn't care; the main thing was the idea that he had acquired this beautiful woman, Levenstein's wife.

5

But not completely.

Once, Cynthia had entered quietly while I was working on the book and stood looking over my shoulder; I remained unaware of her presence (Cynthia wasn't one of your silent movers — often her clinking jewelry worthy of Aida in the opera gave her away), until she remarked, "Your work product looks like it was written by a chicken." "It's only a first draft, "I defended myself. "Another seven should do it," she opined, perhaps peeved that I had bestowed on her a dirty look. She knew I didn't like to be interrupted when working, let alone having my work looked at before it was finished. Pascal said that "all the miserableness of a human being results from his inability to sit quietly alone in his room." Cynthia wasn't one for solitary rooming — nor for letting another engage in the practice. She said, "When Levenstein worked, he didn't like being disturbed. He wanted a companion in what he was doing, not an interloper." That must have been difficult for our prima donna, I mused. Certainly, Levenstein wasn't one for an equivalent role. I couldn't picture him turning her sheet music. On another occasion, Cynthia tiptoed into where I was writing comments re Levenstein's writings and, having observed me silently, startled me with her basso voce. "Your y's are too short; they indicate an excessive humility."

"I plead mea culpa."

"And the miniscule size of the loop in your o's displays introspection."

"Nu, what's new."

"The excessive size in the loop of Levenstein's o's manifests exaggeration and egoism."

"Whose side are you on?" I queried without stopping to think if it was wise. Immediately I realized that it I had erred. I considered softening and saving the situation by a proffered paraphrasing of the Yiddish philosophic query: "If I will be like Levenstein, who will be like me?" But it was too late.

There prevailed a silence pregnant as any in a Harold Pinter play, but perhaps sensing that the fate of Levenstein's book hung in the balance (it didn't), Cynthia opted for kissing me on the back of my neck. Not an answer, a prelude.

6

The reader needs no reminding of Kornfein's tendency to quote from here and there and everywhere. "You bake literary chocolate chip cookies with the chips of other writers," Sandra had put it. Despite borrowing copiously from Kornfein's fund of literary references, Levenstein once damned them as "token trivia." "The middle road is best, Kornfien, the middle road." He removed from Kornfein's reviews most of his "cultural baggage," though he never cured him of his "incorrigible" fondness for them. Kornfein recalled that, on one occasion, Levenstein humorously criticized a review of Kornfein's for its "paucity of references," wondering if Kornfein had suffered some kind of "cultural shock," perhaps induced by Kornfein's imitating the writing style of the writer reviewed, an espouser of the "thin writing" approach which Levenstein did not care for. When Kornfein recalled Levenstein's differing from him on his affinity for references, he felt a pang of guilt because he knew Levenstein wouldn't be happy with his fleshing out of "his" book with such inclusions. Or resurrecting Kornfein's original references which he had pared down. Tit for tat, Kornfein told himself; albeit, uncomfortable at their application. A.L. — After Levenstein.

And there was the day Levenstein had asked him, "Why do you insist on quoting so much from other writers?" Nettled at the question, Kornfein replied from the hip, "Because they write better than me." Levenstein was silent for a moment and then replied softly, "Kornfein, you write well enough." Kornfein cherished the memory.

Not that Levenstein desisted from borrowing Kornfein's literary references when the chief critic deemed that they added clout to the ultimate review which was published under his, Levenstein's, name. His borrowing large sections from Kornfein's writings of which the references were the kernels did not bother Levenstein unduly.

'Not 'plagiarism,' my boy, "unconsious echo"; sometimes "aesthetic borrowing" (the second seemed to Kornfein closer to the mark); other times, farbeserung" (improvement). Levenstein quoted Tennyson: "No man may write a single passage to which a parallel one may not be found in the literature of the world." He pointed out a long list of classical writers beginning with Chaucer who cribbed from Boccaccio up to more modern writers as diverse and esteemed as Coleridge, Faulkner and T.S. Eliot who took a most tolerant approach toward copying others' works. They reasoned that if a writer improved on the original, it was a praiseworthy act in the service of literature. Finnegans Wake proclaimed itself to be "the last word in stolentelling." Levenstein concluded his defense, "I learn from the masters." Kornfein could not gauge if this was an ironic reference to filching from him, or a serious acknowledgment of Coleridge & Co. In any event, Coleridge, Faulkner, T.S. Eliot and Joyce were apparently unaware, or decided to ignore, the Talmudic sages' declaration, "If you quote in the name of a person who said it — you bring redemption to the world."

Levenstien added, "If you steal nuggets of wisdom from one book, you are damned as a plagiarist, but if you steal from ten books, you are called a 'literary researcher,' and from thirty-five books, an 'esteemed researcher.' Of course, if you are an 'esteemed critic '"… he raised his hand palm up to let Kornfein supply his own conclusion.

At times not only 'esteemed critic,' but 'sole esteemed critic.' It still rankled Kornfein that when an international conference on metaphor was held in Tel Aviv some years before (under a banner which proclaimed: "'The richest accumulation of the ages is the noble metaphors we have rolled up.' Robert Frost, beating out Borges: 'It may be that universal history is the history of a handful of metaphors' — in part because the latter was too long, in part because it was too reductionist. Levenstein had attended it alone.

The papers to be delivered at the conference had whetted Kornfein's appetite: "Metaphors in the Bible", "Metaphors and Greek Myth", "Metaphors in the Epic of Gilgamesh", "'All the World's a Stage': Metaphor in Shakespeare's Comedies", "'A Long Noodle': Yiddish Metaphor" — to cite a partial list. Kornfein had been keenly interested in participating, but Lieberman informed him gruffly, "I know your metaphorical nostrils are twitching to attend the conference, but I need you, my second-in-command, to oversee things at the office." Despite the comrade-in arms bestowal, Kornfein felt like Levenstein's custodian rather than his colleague. He was hardly assuaged by his recalling Nietzsche's "Only by forgetting this primitive world of metaphor can one live with any repose, security, and consistency." Nor, when seeing Kornfein's disappointment, Levenstein added, with a momzeric glint in his eye, "The kite of literature cannot rise to the heights if somebody doesn't stand below and hold the string." Kornfein as holder; "literature", or more accurately, its embodiment, Levenstein, as the kite.

Kornfein suspected that Levenstein feared he might outshine him at the conference. Levenstein , for his part, knew that he, Kornfein, was not very sociable at these conferences and also was not built for the required "podium posturing and postulating" whereas he, Levenstein, met the lectern demands, and also the social demands, thanks to his strong intellect, dry humor, and expression of restrained benevolence. Levenstein was also fond of telling literary anecdotes, particularly before or after the conference sessions or at coffee and cake breaks or at the heavier carousing and tale-telling sessions at the academic watering holes (which he dubbed "the irrigated groves of Academe" in a tone of mock reproof), where he had his own private audience. He would recount a spicy tale about Flaubert or Balzac. "Nobody remembers what was said at conferences after a month, but the anecdotes endure," Levenstein told Kornfein.

In this vein, amusing to hear (the first time) was Levensein recounting how, at an international conference on language, Jacques Lacan, the French psychoanalyst and philosopher, gave a presentation on 'the linguistic nature of psychological symptomatology' ("the kind of highfalutin metacrap you like, Kornfein," Levenstein later commented). At one point, Lacan stated that "language was beyond the control of the self", at which point Levenstein exclaimed, "Not in my case," causing those sitting near him, not among the speaker's disciples, to laugh heartily.

Surely at a metaphor conference Levenstein would trot out Proust's dictum: "I think that only metaphor is able to grant to style a kind of eternity, and it seems that in all Flaubert there's not even one beautiful metaphor."

Seemingly the principal thing that Levenstein brought him back from the conference on metaphor was a (true) story which Kornfein delighted in telling whenever in any conversation the subject of metaphor raised its head.

An American professor on his way to the conference was interviewed by Israeli security personnel during check-in for a flight to Tel Aviv. When asked why he was flying to Tel Aviv, he replied that he had been invited to a conference on metaphor. The interviewer asked, "What's a metaphor?" When the professor hesitated, momentarily at a loss for words, the interviewer asked sharply, "You're going to a metaphor conference and you don't even know what a metaphor is?" The professor was thereupon hustled away by security guards and interrogated for almost an hour before one of the conference hosts, an Israeli professor from the University of Tel Aviv, intervened and vouched for his legitimacy.

7

We find Kornfein in Cynthia's bath. Since he began working on her late husband's book, he had "carte blanche" (in Cynthia's words) to her apartment, subject to the condition that he always telephone prior to coming. She turned down his suggestion that she give him a duplicate key.

Cynthia once told him, "I enjoy the bath since it is a pleasure to gaze at my naked body. Those who don't have a beautiful body should take a shower and finish the business faster." "Such as yours truly," he had shot back, thinking the barb aimed at him. She laughed, declining to elaborate, dissembling by poking him with her prehensile toes.

Kornfein's pleasure in thinking in the bath was interrupted by Cynthia's entering the room, angry about something to judge from the hard-set of her features; when hard-set, her usually impressive features looked like a mask out of Japanese kabuki theater or the mother-in-law in Yiddish theater.

Cynthia possessed high fallutin notions of art — despite which she had hung a singularly amateurish painting in the hallway which she had received as a gift from a "good friend" (gender not disclosed nor did Kornfein press the matter) who, she said, "insisted I hang it as a precondition for receiving it." It portrayed what seemingly was an elderly lady (or young alien) all in black set against an urban background. The painter's or the giver's mother, Kornfein mused. He did not trouble Cynthia with his musings. He contented himself with characterizing the thing as "mishigothic" (a definition borrowed from Billy Wilder) and titling it "Whistler's Mother — on a Bad Day." He couldn't resist laying this onto Cynthia, who became indignant.

On another occasion, it was Cynthia in the bath, not Kornfein. He didn't know that she was going to be in the bath. What happened — as she explained to him afterward — was that she was in a particularly good mood, something to do with a "glowing harp review" (her words) of her performance published in some small musical journal. It apparently stimulated her libido because when Kornfein arrived on a visit (after phoning first, of course) in order to plow through some more of Levenstein's work product, he found a note on the door written in Cynthia's calligraphic script (truly beautiful when she chose to take pains to write it): "Catch me if you can", and under it the harp sketch which she sometimes drew as a logo. Kornfein remembered that Socrates, before his death, had said something to this effect, but obviously Cynthia had something else in mind.

He tried the door. It was unlocked. This surprised him because Cynthia had an obsession with locked doors, even when Levenstein was alive. One night, Levenstein forgot his key. She was asleep, and he spent considerable time ringing and knocking until she woke up. Kornfein once asked her about this over-concern with locked doors. "My harp," she explained. "Somebody might steal my harp." Picturing somebody struggling to make off with her harp caused him to chuckle. "Don't laugh," she had upbraided him. "It has been known to happen." There was more to it than that, of course, Kornfein reasoned. Maybe she didn't want to be caught in medias res with a suitor. The idea filled him with jealousy.

Entering the apartment, Kornfein looked for her first of all in the salon

(A new sofa, or perhaps a couch, whose opulent, filigreed upholstery, even taken in at a cursory glance, got on his nerves. Not so much Fen Shi as Late Darius. He could picture Sandra shaking her head at it — or laughing). He then looked for her in the kitchen, and from there in the bedroom. No Cynthia. But draped on her bed was a shiny leather mouse-brown jacket; alongside it, a leather shoulder bag of eggplant purple. A pair of matching purple stilettoed-heeled shoes had seemingly been kicked off in haste; they lay on the floor next to the bed, one shoe on its side.

This fetching set of accessories Kornfein had never seen before. Their late mode styling and obvious expensiveness told him they did not stem from the Levensteinic era. Perhaps love-tokens of a suitor. Kornfein then noticed a vase of narcissuses, yellow and white and pink, on the table near her bed. Maybe the gift of the same (or worse, a different) suitor, Kornfein could not help but suspecting; however, he then remembered that Cynthia liked narcissuses and perchance it was she who had purchased them. Ordinarily, Cynthia's premises lacked flowers of any kind, as if she didn't have the time or patience for them. Kornfein remembered that he once asked her about this. "They give off oxygen'" she explained. "That's healthy," he had replied. "So they say," she said, without further explanation. He had then decided not to pursue the matter, her tone having increased in volume, a sure sign of her dissatisfaction with their little tête-à-tête.

And this memory about flowers triggered off another: the time that Levenstein, displeased at a review that he, Kornfein, had written that failed to come up to his expectations, observed, "You should have been a greeting-card writer, Kornfein, writing about flowers and butterflies, but your flowers would come out faded and your butterflies, moths. Write about bees, Kornfein — add a bit of sting." 'Stung' by Levenstein's going too far, he had answered him, "You take on the carnivores, Saul, I'll stick with the herbivores." Levenstein looked at Kornfein for a long moment, apparently unsure (for once) how to respond. "Fair enough," he said finally, seemingly pleased by his response, or maybe the fact that he had responded at all. When Kornfein told Sandra about his 'triumph', she snorted," The herbivores don't stand a chance against the carnivores." Sometime afterward, following one of his losing battles with Cynthia, Sandra's words came back to him.

But let us return to Cynthia in her fetching mood. She must have heard him open the door or prowling around (she was blessed with good ears, equipment vital for a musician). "In here," he heard her exasperated voice say.

The voice came from the bathroom. That was where she wanted him to "catch" her? He thought of Actaeon who, according to the charming Greek myth, surprised the goddess Diana while she was bathing naked and who was turned into a stag in punishment and torn to pieces by his own dogs. Tiresias fared slightly better than Actaeon: he was blinded by Athena after he stumbled onto her bathing naked. (And they say Jews have an angry God.)

Entering the bathroom, he found his naiad in her bubbled bath, naked as Venus emerging from the foamy waves in Botticelli's painting. Cynthia was lying, her upper body above the water, her arms crossed in front of her chest in the style of Egyptian pharaohs depicted in temple paintings. Cynthia constituted, without doubt, an adornment to the bath.

Kornfein stared at her blankly. She raised her hands and shook them like a belly dancer (or maybe Salome in her famous dance). "Queen of the Bathtub," she announced in good spirits.

He didn't know what was expected of him.

She told him. "Come join me," she said in a voluptuous whisper, extending her arms toward him in invitation. She wore her cat-that-stole-the-cream smile. Her eyes bore into him with Kama Sutra seductiveness.

"Get undressed?" he inquired of her.

She lowered her arms in exasperation. "People usually do before they enter the bath."

It dawned on him that she wasn't interested in his cleanliness.

"It's not my style," he informed her. It wasn't.

She glowered at him. "You and Sandra never...?"

Nu, and her and Levenstein in the bath tub. Kornfein shut his mind to the thought.

Her invasion of his privacy rankled. Kornfein said nothing. His saying nothing in turn rankled her. "How about on the threshing house floor?" she taunted. He felt like the Golem of Prague confronted by Abishag or Jezabel.

She began to check a glistening leg for appearing veins. When she appeared to find one, his would-be-appeasing "inlaid marble" failed to appease her, earning him a dismissive snort.

Given Cynthia's mood, Kornfein decided retreat was the prudent course. He would go work on the book. As he left the bathroom, pursued by his inamorata's heaped honorifics: "zeide, schlemiel, schlimazel" followed by "Ikh hob dikh in bod" (To hell with you) — once again, the diva-dame in one of her groyser kundes (big stick) moods; Diotoma, Socrates' love-instructress, had become Xanthippe, Socrates' shrewish wife, Yiddish curses having replaced Greek ones. At that moment he appreciated the overheard sentiment once muttered by Levenstein, "I am not married to a woman; I'm married to a temperament."

He feared being struck by an object from her Venetian glass collection, perhaps the kitsch (in his eyes) dolphin which lay on a glass shelf in arm's reach of the bathtub. Why, Kornfein reflected, couldn't I have a mistress like that of Herzog in Bellow's (eponymous) novel who is kind and beautiful and has a religion of sex which she believes can cure Herzog's ailments? Yet he knew by now that such a mistress's cure, however kind and well-intended, might only add to his own ailments.

He retreated from the wrath of the caladarium to the inner sanctum of the scriptorium, having considered but immediately rejected taking a parting shot at Cynthia, like the Parthians who fired arrows over their shoulder while retreating from battle. He recalled that Cynthia said to him once, "You always seem as if you are looking for an escape route." This remark had struck him as uncharacteristically astute. It, or his present predicament, conjured up before his eyes Cigoli's painting "Jospeh and Potiphar's Wife' together with the biblical inspiration for it: And she caught him by his robe saying, "lie with me" and he left his garment in her hand, and fled. He wondered if his passivity was not a goad to Cynthia.

Safely in his work-room, he began turning over one by one the items of Levenstein's corpus, so insulted and incensed that he paid no attention to what was written on them. The imagined picture of Cynthia and Levenstein naked in the bath pursued him.

After some minutes Cynthia's throat voice, softer, called him. The softness decided him despite his knowledge that when Cynthia was being overly sweet a threat hung in the air; Kornfein had always been a patsy for softness, for heindelach. He put aside his being miffed, his being the klutz, his hors de combat status and, returning to the bath room, entered.

She was still in the bath tub, looking like nothing so much as a pouting seal whose ball had fallen from its nose during a performance. Suddenly she stood up, extending her arms invitingly toward him. "Come on, Kornfein, let go of your poor-little-boy mood. I only wanted to surprise you," Cynthia purred honey-voiced. "Give me a hug."

Kornfein redux. He complied, despite thoroughly soaking his shirt and pants in the process; as he did so, he reflected that Cynthia's sudden change of moods, like the wiles of Catullus' mistress, caused him irritation and admiration in equal measure. And he berated himself for being so dependent on the whims of others — Levenstein for sure, Cynthia without doubt (as in the present instance), even Sandra, perhaps? Cynthia got out of the tub, her magnificent body dripping water. Not inferior to the sultan's favorite in the painting 'The Sultan's Favorite Returning from the Bath'. My Galatea, thought Kornfein, favoring the Greek conception of feminine beauty to the Ottomanic's over-amplitude in the thighs. Cynthia did not hurry to wrap herself in a towel. "Take off your clothes. I will dry them for you. Put on the robe." (Levenstein's robe.) Kornfein obeyed. As he donned the robe, a question nagged at him: Am I taking part in the tribal ritual of slaying the father?

He wondered if for him sex with Cynthia had become monotonous (long since fled the stimulating image of himself as calf embraced by an anaconda). He recalled that when De Maupassant complained to Flaubert that sex was becoming monotonous, the elder writer urged his disciple to cut it out for a while. Alas, Cynthia would never take such advice if Kornfein proffered it, which he dared not do: he had suffered enough Yiddish curses for one day.

Not in the bathtub, not on the threshing room floor. On the bed. Levenstein's corpus could wait. For once, Cynthia didn't urge him to work on the book. A rarity, nonetheless welcome for being so.

Their 'reconciliation' was carried out to the notes of Beethoven's piano sonata in F minor, the 'Appassionata', which Cynthia had deftly put on her disc player, the music expressing love, passion, doubt, pain and purification.

8

The day came when I threw down the manuscript. "I can do no more,"

I said out loud to myself. From the other room I heard Cynthia's voice, "Did you say something, Kornfein?"

I wanted to reply at the top of my voice, "Say? Did!" but thought better of being too triumphant. Cynthia cherished triumphs solely of her own making. And yet, maybe my triumph — completing Levenstein's book

— was hers as well. I felt suddenly sad rather than triumphant. And I wondered if there wasn't something prescient in this feeling. Or was it simply a literary equivalent of post-coital depression.

So the book was finished. I recalled Pushkin's description of the moment he finished Boris Godunov: "I read it aloud, alone, and clapped my hands and cried, "Well done, Pushkin, well done, you son-of-a-bitch!"

That's what I could envision Levenstein uttering as critic on High, though we would likely substitute for "son of a bitch," momzer." Nor did I weigh the manuscript in my palm and murmur a "Well, well," as did Nabokov's Hermann on the completion of his novel. I adopted a more laconic response: "This is the best I can do at this time."

9

A radio 'books' program invited both Cynthia and myself to be jointly interviewed as "Levenstein's closest associates" (she as the late critic's wife, me as his right hand) as the radio hostess generously put it in introducing us to her listeners. Cynthia had tried strenuously to limit the "closest associates" to one — herself, but she met her match in the radio hostess, a woman who had once been a teacher and so had faced pressure before. Nevertheless, Cynthia managed to take over the lion's share of commentary — even launching into an unstoppable paen to harp playing, particularly her own, when the hostess commented on a reference to harp-playing in the book, a reference I hadn't noted in going over the book, and now I wonder if Cynthia hadn't inserted it after I had corrected the last proofs, particularly as it was a kind of roman-à-clef inclusion leaving little doubt as to the true identity of the harp virtuoso; and I further wondered if Cynthia had even gone so far as to plant the harp question of the hostess together with her in the ladies room prior to the broadcast. In short, Cynthia attempted to conduct a tour around a pedestal — Levenstein; albeit that Cynthia was less interested in Levenstein as pedestal than in Cynthia as Woman Behind/Responsible for the Pedestal. Out of politeness, respect for the dead, and fear of Cynthia, I did not clarify the picture. In short, a nebbish.

The Kornfein-as-nebbish aspect Cynthia did nothing to diminish, and even encouraged, perhaps guided by the tactics that the more I looked bad, the better she would look. She hinted that I was a dabbler, a dilettante, as opposed to Levenstein, or even herself! For example, her reference to the book as "a work worthy of Kornfein's reputation," on her lips sounded more like criticism than praise. Particularly as she then launched into a spiel about all the sparkle, wit, and wisdom that Levenstein brought to the book, then mentioning (in dismissive coda) my "editing" of it. Not content with disparaging my herculean contribution to the book, she turned to ad hominem attack, bringing up what she denigrated as my "cheapness" (Sandra, my ex-wife, had used "parsimony", I preferred "frugality"), that I insisted on walking whenever we went anywhere together — even here (to the studio—it was true), never taking a cab (she wouldn't hear of taking a bus). I did not rejoin that Cynthia lamented the passing of the sedan chair. And when the radio hostess asked her at one point, "To which moment in your life would you like to return?" assuming, perhaps, she would mention some brilliant harp recital or an endearing moment with her late husband, Cynthia paused significantly before answering, "To the moment before I met Kornfein."

I should have been on guard from the moment I first saw her in the studio. (Cynthia had glided into it, in marked contrast to my own halting ingress, uncomfortable with the whole idea of an interview, let alone a joint interview with Cynthia in which she would engage in her favorite topic — herself.) She was dressed in what I thought of as her "Henry VIII mode" in which she summoned up the combination of splendor and menace found in the famous Holbein portrait of Henry, conveyed best in the expression, 'Dressed to kill.' And the words "You are sometimes a bit ridiculous, Kornfein," came to me. I couldn't recall the occasion or the context in which Cynthia had uttered them, but did recall thinking: even Levenstein, in his greatest moments of disapproval, never used that word. And now I was struck with the thought that all the problems in my relationship with Cynthia began then. And Cynthia was likely unaware of it. Or if aware, uncaring. And I knew that during the studio interview to come Cynthia was capable of providing information which was in part true, in part imagined, and in part fabricated, intermixed with bouts of false enthusiasm punctuated by her overly robust, operatic laugh.

Cynthia had embraced me, not out of affection, but as a means of whispering in my ear, "Kornfein, remember that the public does not want to hear about you, but to hear about Levenstein."

As I was digesting this remark, she added, "I hope you won't be unpleasant."

Me? Unpleasant? I thought of a character in a story by Robert Walser who says that somebody who thinks a lot becomes unpleasant — or is thought of as unpleasant. I had always considered myself as pleasant, or at least not unpleasant. "You think I'm unpleasant?" I challenged her.

"Don't think about it too much," she replied.

"Nu?" I persisted, stung by her suggestion, even though I suspected that it might have been a deliberate tactic on her part to put me on the defensive.

"Mildly pleasant," she replied. "At times. On occasion." After a pause, "On this occasion, I hope."

Cynthia employed her pauses even more significantly during the interview. A shtick of hers, taken, I assumed, from the Yiddish theatre which she liked to attend, so that every word of hers that went out over the airways would be significant, with me her hoped-for silent partner. I was reminded, however unlikely the comparison, of St. Teresa who kept a stenographer at her side so that comments from her ecstasies would always be suitable for publication. Cynthia had ecstasies of her own.

My pauses were usually induced by a lack of some-thing to say on my part or a failure to respond to some snide remark on Cynthia's part directed toward, or about, me — for instance: "Say something profound, Kornfein" or "Kornfein is the consummate scribe." She meant to Levenstein. Did the listeners grasp this or, hopefully, think she was praising him? As I wrestled with these possibilities, Cynthia had moved on to pro-viding free psychoanalysis of me over the air waves, "Kornfein's problem is that he wants everyone to be nice to him. That's why he writes." Oddly, Levenstein once said something to the same effect.

Sometimes Cynthia seized on a pause of mine to begin and continue with one of her spiels, though her favored tactic was, again, the barb. "Kornfein is think-ing. Kornfein likes to think. Other people breathe. Kornfein thinks." This caused me to remember, on the day of Levenstein's interviewing me for the position of literary assistant when I was on pins and needles as to whether I would be accepted for the position, there ensued a long silence following which Levenstein leaned forward in his chair, placed his hands flat on the desk in front of him, and finally spoke. "It is evident that you think seriously about serious literary matters and, above all — that you think!" upon which he extended his hand in confirmation of my acceptance. I of course refrained from defending my 'thinking' by thus using the late-so-lamented-by-Cynthia-Levenstein to counter his wife lest she accuse me of bad taste or worse irreverence toward the subject we had been invited to discuss.

And yet all this "thinking" business caused me to recall the time Levenstein spied me, as he passed my cubicle, sitting deep in thought. "Kornfein, you look perplexed. Go read Maimonides." He was referring to Maimonides' book 'Guide for the Perplexed' — because of its title. Levenstein was big on titles. He liked to rename famous books with new humorous titles, such as, 'Albertine of Sunnybrook Farm' for 'Rememberance of Things Past'. Such "improved" titles he would trot out in order to entertain the review's staff at our annual office Purim party. They went down better with red wine.

At other times Cynthia employed to good effect her machine-gun speech when angry or determined to make her point, a potent verbal weapon which covered up her sometimes shaky assertions. One that was not shaky: "Kornfein doesn't realize that telling is enough, explaining, too much." Not bad, I thought, though offended. Less successful, perhaps, her "All Kornfein does is read, write, and read." Pause, then, "Kornfein spends too much time in his own head. Even when he sleeps." At this latter hint of contiguity, I blushed — the radio listeners couldn't see it, and I hoped the interviewer didn't notice, but I was sure Cynthia noticed. On the one hand, her hint at physical contact between us would fly in the face of her All-Levenstein stance; on the other, it fit her dramatic love to shock. Stung by her sallies, I left off such musing and shot back, "There is hardly enough interview time at my disposal to succeed in portraying all the nuances of behavior and peccadilloes of the Lady (here I nodded at Cynthia, despite the radio audience's inability to see it), though 'nuances' is too nuanced a word to apply to her." She didn't know whether I was praising her or defaming her but suspecting the latter, lashed into me.

Cynthia: "Kornfein is so touchy."

Kornfein: "Me? Touchy?"

Cynthia: "You. Touchy. Like now."

During our mutual review (in theory—she monopolized most of the time) I received a number of cold stares from Cynthia whenever I said something less than praiseworthy in her eyes. Even on those rare occasions when the hostess succeeded in addressing a question clearly to me (during my answers Cynthia would pluck a rugelach from the plate placed for guests and chew it noisily, perhaps hoping to 'jam' my presentation; the sugar dusted pieces lined with cinnamon and raisins and walnuts were a favorite of hers), I was acutely conscious that Cynthia (despite her vigorous ingesting) was following with prehensile attention each word of my answer, even surreptitiously taking my hand on one occasion and squeezing it in warning when she decided that I was getting dangerously close to (unconsciously?) commenting on the book in such a way as might indicate a too-close knowledge of a certain aspect that should have been exclusively that of the author. To disabuse any listener of such a nefarious notion, she abandoned my hand and, discarding her hitherto aggressive faux charm approach in favor of the aggressive dramatic, raised the book in both hands high above her head (surely regretting that the radio audience was deprived of the sight, but they could hear her and to insure it she ratcheted up a notch the intensity of her voice): "This book is the flesh and the blood of Levenstein!" "He is risen," I wanted to chime in, but of course did not. (Years later looking back I sometimes regret not having suddenly announced that I had actually written the principal part of the book. But I was not Levenstein.)

On a second occasion when Cynthia decided that I had strayed from the true path (of deception) — she winced when I quoted Flaubert to the effect that success when it came, always struck for the wrong reason, a bit of innocuous innuendo, in my opinion — she actually kicked me in the shin. I was struck by the vision of Lotte Lenya as the SPECTRE agent in the movie 'From Russia with Love' trying to kick James Bond with a pair of shoes equipped with switchblade knives. Cynthia's 'prod' caused me, in order to throw off any suspicions that my literary bagatelle might otherwise raise, to utter a series of non-sequitors to what I had been saying.

That night, in recompense for my dissembling, Cynthia (naked) kissed my blackened shin, thereafter adding that she was sure that Sandra had never "kissed my wounds". I felt like Jesus being spoiled by Mary of Bethany (if Mary Magdalene was closer to Cynthia)

— or maybe she had only washed his feet, so that I was one up, so to speak. But I will not dwell here on my wound as did Homer upon Philoctetes' wound, interrupting the plot of 'The Iliad' to devote 70 lines to his ailment and kvetching. My few lines are sufficient given our more impatient age. "No, Sandra never did," I admitted, with a certain modicum of shame, since Sandra had never wounded me to the extent that she, Cynthia, had. I refrained from pointing this out, fearing my bringing up Sandra might destroy the mood of such rare tenderness on the part of Cynthia, which I hoped would lead to kissing of more than shins, which it did. During her physical ministrations, I felt like a male prostitute being paid for my 'good behavior' during the interview.

10

But apparently, Cynthia's appreciation went beyond that of rewarding me physically for my good behavior at the book interview. It seems that publication of the book freed Cynthia, as well as me, from Levenstein. "Kornfein, now that the book is finished, I no longer need you. But I have learned that I want you. You are a less renowned critic than Levenstein, yet a more empathic person. You care about me, something that Levenstein rarely showed. What's more, I have become used to you, with all your eccentricities. I'm getting too old for suitors. Yes, I know that you knew. I invite you to move in with me, permanently, Korn. You no longer have to call me first. Since you are so, ah, frugal, it will save you money in telephone bills. And if there is a second printing of Levenstein's book, I have decided to list you as co-author. Some literary critics suspect the fact, anyhow, so we might as well come clean."

I was flabbergasted. Cynthia and the book, in one breathless offer.

Hugging me, Cynthia told me, "Now you belong to me, and no longer do I have to share you with the book."

For the first time, I felt I had replaced Levenstein in Cynthia's life.

Yiddish Glossary
Larry Lefkowitz and Avram Patt

A hon nokh tashmish – A rooster after the hens have been served.

A rooster that doesn't follow the wisdom: the egg of today is better than the hen of tomorrow. He follows the precept: The hen of today is better than the egg at any time.

Speaking of chickens, a philosophical haiku in the Yiddish idiom:
The chicken of life
Is by the shochet breasted
The stuffing remains
("Shochet" is ritual slaughterer.)

Abi men zeht zikh – He was only himself.
Or as Laurence Harvey, the actor, once put it, "Some of my best moments are spent with me."

As long as I'm up here, there's another story I'd like to tell you. I was once working late in the offices of the Attorney General of New Jersey, and the Attorney General himself was escorting someone around to show him the premises. The Attorney General opened the door to my office, looked in saw me, and told the other fellow, "There's no one here."

Apposite, the Yiddish saying, Az ich vel zayn vi er, ver vet zayn vi ich? If I am going to be like him, who will be like me?

Aroyskrikhn zoln dir di oygn fun kop – May your eyes crawl out of your head.

Aoyb ir lebn lang genug epes kenen pasirn – If you live long enough anything can happen.

After years of unsuccessful blind and seeing dates (one told him "I expected a date, not a fig"), so many blind dates that after five years he found himself matched with the same dates he had before, he finally found his match ordained in heaven. According to the wise Talmudic expression, "Find wife, find good." Edgar Alan Poe surmised that the original expression was "find wife, find a good woman." Apparently, Poe never found a nice Jewish girl or his writing would have been less gloomy and more Yiddishkeit. He would have written "Meeting Sheila in the Catskills" and not "Annabel Lee."

Beltsh – belch.
After a beltsh, when you get a disparaging look, don't excuse yourself; say, ven ikh ess, hob ikh zey ale drerd: When I eat, they can all go to hell.
Berd – medium length beard.
There is also the berdinke, berdinkelle, berdinyunkele.

Berdl – closed cropped beard.

Bord – lengthy dignified beard.
Mendele Mocher sforim said, "Better a Jew without a

beard, than a beard without a Jew."

Drek – rubbish, trash, excrement.

Vashti wrote: Dear Diary, I finally did it, telling that toad, Ahasuerus, where to get off, and who to get off of. Summoning me like some kitchen wench whenever he gets the urge, usually so drunk he can't tell a Mede from a Persian. And then I have to cool my heels and anything else that might have been inflamed until till he raises that damned scepter of his. Even that he raises a lot faster than his other scepter, which falls short of the mark.

Ikh bin dir moykhl – I forgive you.

Genghis Cohen (he changed it to Genghis Kahn so he could marry a divorcee) in his memoirs stated that the moment he saw the Great wall of China, he wanted wall-to-wall carpeting. "Unfortunately, the other wall was on the Danube. I had to settle for linoleum in the end as the Persians couldn't come up with a big enough carpet. The linoleum impeded our conquests for a time. My mother had just washed it and my warriors were slipping all over the place. And the horses were spread-eagled. I didn't speak to my mother for a week. She didn't speak to me for a month – for getting all our ten thousand footprints on it after she had cleaned."

Es zol dir dunern in boykh un blitzen in di hoyzn – You should have thunder in your belly and lightening in your pants. At least she spared him, zol dir lign in keyver der eyver, in dikishkes a lokh mit a sheyver -May

your penis lie in a grave, a hole and a hernia in your guts.
Fortzele – fart.
After passing wind, one can employ the above response.
Or say, "The company is so special and the conversation
so sparkling, I didn't want to go and miss both by sitting
on the toilet."

Galitzianer – one from Galicia located in western Ukraine
and southeastern Poland. Hungary, as part of Austro-
Hungary was part of Galicia. My father liked to joke, "Every
Hungarian recipe begins the same, 'First you steal a potato.'"

Groyser kundes – big stick
Jewish humor favors the ironic, unlike Israeli humor
which tends more to the direct and often the clownish.
A Jewish humorist in Israel (read: me) feels like Ruth
among the alien corn.
    Theodore Roosevelt said, "Speak softly and carry a
big stick." If he was Jewish, he would have urged, "Speak
up and carry a big shtick."

Heindelakh – softness.
Ad in National Lampoon: Orthodox psychologist who
knows how to live well seeks sympathetic woman to
share bleeding ulcer.

Ikh hob dikh in bod – To hell with you.
Issac Rosenfeld and Saul Bellow parodied T.S. Eliot's
'The Love Song of J. Alfred Prufrock.' Their version

inspired others, including me. I don't know if Eliot read or was displeased by the Yiddish. No matter, he was an anti-Semite. Here two examples:
(original) I grow old … I grow old …
I shall wear the bottoms of my trousers rolled.
Ikh ver alt, ikh ver alt
Un der pupik vert mir kalt.
I grow old …I grow old …
And my pupik gets cold.
In the room the women come and go
Talking of Michelangelo.
The last line becomes: Speaking of Marx and Lenin
(The line ends rhyme in the Yiddish.)

In drerd arayn – Should be buried in the ground.
The director of an actor who died young delivered a funeral speech: "It was *I* who first noticed your great talent. *I* who gave you your first stage contract. It was *I* in whose theatre you achieved your promising successes. Ultimately, it was on the stage of *my* theatre that you established your fame." At this moment the corpse sat up, "Excuse me, sir, but who is being buried here, you or I."

Inzikhist – the introspective. A type like Oscar Levant who explained that success made him feel so "guilty" that whenever he watched a courtroom drama on television and the accused stood up, he stood up also.

Or like the Jewish patient (in Leo Rosten's classic joke) who sent a picture postcard from vacationing in

Barbados, "Having a wonderful time. Why?"

Ketzele – kitten, little kitten.

When their sex declined from the "oi" on her part to the "meh," the death knell on her part: Mir darfn farsheydnkayt, "We need variety." He tried using techniques from 'Fifty Shades of Grey,' but her " tandeneh arbeit," "botched work," put an end to their relationship.

Kroynele – darling dear.

The above endearments have been cited as the real reason for Mona Lisa's smile. Her real name was Mona Lisa Siegelbaum and she was a sucker for khnife-flattery in Yiddish. Leonardo Da Vinci tried Italian endearments at first, but switched to Yiddish ones when she refused to smile. His 'The Last Supper' was inspired at a Passover meal with Mona's parents, after which, he was reputed to have declared, "That's the last supper I will attend with Mona's parents, matzahs are hell on my digestive system." He did come up with the concept of square matzah-balls for his flying machine trays.

Leydikgeyer – a good for nothing.

On the subject of nothing. At the end of his prayer, the cantor added, "Lord of the universe, I am nothing." The rabbi said, "Lord, I am less than nothing." When the shammas, the sexton, said, "I, too, am nothing, O Lord, the rabbi turned to the cantor, dismissably, "Look who thinks he's a nothing!"

In a Jewish theological seminary, a discussion took

place about the proofs of the existence of god. Finally, tired of all the discussion, a rabbi said, "God is so great, He doesn't even need to exist."

Makher – Big shot.
In the dental students' wing of the Hebrew University, among the plaques of donors, is one which will warm the heart of any lover of Yiddish: "This dental clinic donated by his wife in loving memory of _______ Yiddish author and oral surgeon." Note the order of importance.

Maven – expert.
A scout rushed into the clubhouse of the baseball team (that was floundering in last place) and up to the manager. "I just saw a kid in a sand-lot game strike out 27 batters in a row. He had such baffling curves and blinding speed that nobody got a foul off him till two were out in the ninth. Should I sign him up?" "You're balmy," the manager told him. "It's hitters we need right now. Sign the fellow who got the foul off him."

Eddie Cantor became friendly with Will Rogers, cowboy humorist. "The cowboy was the first guy I'd ever met from west of the Bronx and I worshiped him. I bought him his first kosher meal." Cantor's Yiddish phrasing and rhythms became a hallmark of Jewish humor. Years later, at a dinner given by the Jewish Theatrical Guild to honor Cantor, Rogers made a speech in pure Yiddish for twenty minutes, then translated it. Cantor said it was the nicest thing anyone ever did for me." Yes, a shayner goy (a beautiful goy – a goy with sterling qualities).

Makhnshpiler – A player of parts.
He was a player of parts, her poopikl, her tsitskes, but never succeeded in arriving to her oyse mokem – the-you-know-where. He knew where but didn't have a GPS to find it.

Momzer – (slang) a bastard, rascal.
(True story published in Jerusalem Post): A Jewish girl in America met and fell in love with a non-Jewish boy. Her family insisted that they would only consent to the wedding if he converted, and so he began studying with a rabbi. As time went on, he became more and more immersed in Judaism and he finally went to Israel to complete his conversion. Eventually she received a letter from Israel. He was sorry, he wrote, but he had to break off the match. He could not marry someone who would have even considered marrying a non-Jew.

Nebish – pitifully ineffectual, timid, submissive. and his brother, the nebech- a nobody.
I was a nebech until I succeeded in becoming a ley-dekgeyer. Then I married and was saved. "Find wife, find good," indeed.

Nu – the most useful of words. Literally, "now." Figuratively, "so, so what"; "and?"; "yes?"; "what am I supposed to do about it"; "therefore?"

Allen Ginsberg, while in the New York State Psychiatric Institute, met Carl Solomon. Their first exchange: Solomon: "Who are you?" Ginsberg: "I'm Myshkin." Solomon: "I'm Kirilov." From that moment their friendship started. Myshkin is the idiot in Dostoyevsky's "The Idiot" (he ends his life in a Swiss asylum) while Kirilov is one of the possessed characters in Dostoyevsky's "The Possessed".

Sometimes diverse cultures meet. The heroic samurai Benkei, according to Japanese legend, killed a giant carp which had swallowed his mother when she fell into a waterfall. It is not recorded if Benkei lost his taste for gefilte fish or sushi. The Japanese legendary monster, the *Nu*, was slain by a samurai no less brave than Benkei. Benkei, disappointedly, is apparently not Japanese affectionate for Benjamin. A Yiddish version would have substituted "mother-in-law" for "mother" and worked in the Yiddish for "Adam was fortunate – he didn't have a mother-in-law."

The ultimate "Nu?": Gertrude Stein, dying, asked "What is the question?"

Nudnik – nag.

According to biological classification, only the Vertebrata have produced Nudniks. We should not be entirely surprised by this fact as the Vertebrata are distinguished by a backbone of vertebrae and two pair of limbs. The limbs are needed for gesturing, an implicit adjunct to nudnikism, and standing is necessary for effective nudnikism, since a lying down Nudnik is ineffective unless he or she is visiting you for some weeks and adopts this position as part of his/her strategy.

Cleopatra nudged in hieroglyphics, which required nudging from right to left, left to right, down to up, and up to down. She was thus a consummate nudnik since she could come at you from all sides. Her failure at nudging Mark Anthony apparently caused her to turn to the asp.

Oytzer – Sweetheart, dear. *(literal translation is "treasure")*

Oyzlozn di gantse toykhekhe – to pile curse after curse into someone.

Pupik – belly button. A gezunt dir in pupik. A blessing meaning good health to your belly button, but means, your whole system should stay healthy.

New York Hebrew uses it in the expression, "Don't jump over your belly button." Don't overreach.

Kobi Mamon became the high jump champion of Israel precisely because he disregarded the admonition.

Shem zikh nit – Don't be bashful
A young woman complained about being a female tourist in Italy. She said that all the men tried to pick her up – even a policeman who followed her around. She should have called a criminal.

Hinde Ena Burstin: "Yiddish is a great language for writing erotic poetry. It has such zaftig, squishy sounds:

oys, oohs, and aahs that are unafraid to be exposed with gusto and with passion" She didn't know how to translate "moaning with pleasure" in Yiddish. There were two options: mruken (a purring moan) and brumen (roaring). She asked the poet she translated which she preferred. Her answer: "Honey, I roar."

Shlemiel – fool

An Orthodox Jew converted to Catholicism and was invited to preach the Sunday Sermon. He stood up proudly and began: "Fellow goyim."

Menasha Skulnik, an actor in Yiddish theater, on Broadway and Uncle David on the television program 'The Goldbergs.' He described himself: "I pay a shlemiel, a dope. Sometimes they call me the Yiddish Charlie Chaplin, and I don't like this. Chaplin's dope is a little bit of a wiseguy. He's got a little larceny in him. I am poor shlemiel, with no strings attached."

I remember, as a youth, seeing Skulnik perform in a play. I don't remember its name, but what I do remember is his repeated shtick. He would raise his hands and say "Not this way, "(in Yiddish?), then lower them and say "This way"; i.e., not big, settle for small. The audience waited with expectation for this delivery and would join in.

Schlimazal – unlucky or inept person who fails at everything.

A **shmendrik** is lowdown in the pantheon of **klutzes**, one up from the **shlemiel**.

Tsitskes – Breasts.

On my dates, rarely did I get to the twin treasures. But then in my day, I considered myself a winner if I got a good-night kiss. Those were the days before 'Fifty shades of Gray.' Color me a stud manque.

When I finally got a girlfriend, she was like a lulav-you could take her for seven days, but then you had to put her away for the rest of the year.

Yekke – a Jew of German-speaking origin, notable for attention to detail and punctuality.

What's the difference between a yekke and a virgin? A yekke remains a yekke.

A gentleman ho immigrated to Israel in the 1930's ordered new office furniture. One chair had one leg shorter than the other three. He called the carpenter, who studied the matter for a moment and said, "I can't understand you. All this time you're going on about this one short leg, and not one word about the other three which are perfectly fine."

Zaftig – a buxom young woman, a moyd vi a tzimmes. Bartalina Shloshberg, the supermodel, was zaftig. Jewish fashion buyers didn't go in for the thin look. Beside an impressive tuchus, she possessed luminescent eyes, lips like the curve of Bear Mountain's summit, a nose straight and smooth as an ivory tower, breasts like twin Catskill Mountains that sloped down to a belly flat as the beach at the Jersey shore. She was into Whitman, and when she murmured, "Flaunt of the sunshine and need not your bask – lie over!" he did.

Fomite

Writing a review on social media sites for readers will help the progress of independent publishing. To submit a review, go to the book page on any of the sites and follow the links for reviews. Books from independent presses rely on reader-to-reader communications.

More story collections from Fomite...

MaryEllen Beveridge — After the Hunger
MaryEllen Beveridge — Permeable Boundaries
Jay Boyer — Flight
L. M Brown — Treading the Uneven Road
L. M Brown — Were We Awake
Michael Cocchiarale — Here Is Ware
Michael Cocchiarale — Still Time
Neil Connelly — In the Wake of Our Vows
Catherine Zobal Dent — Unfinished Stories of Girls
Zdravka Evtimova — Carts and Other Stories
John Michael Flynn — Off to the Next Wherever
Derek Furr — Semitones
Derek Furr — Suite for Three Voices
Elizabeth Genovise — Where There Are Two or More
Andrei Guriuanu — Body of Work
Zeke Jarvis — In A Family Way
Arya Jenkins — Blue Songs in an Open Key
Bobby Johnston — The Saint I Ain't
Jan English Leary — Skating on the Vertical
Julia MacDonnell— The Topography of Hidden Stories
Marjorie Maddox — What She Was Saying
William Marquess — Badtime Stories
William Marquess — Because Because Because Because Because
William Marquess — Boom-shacka-lacka
William Marquess — Things I Want You to Do
Gary Miller — Museum of the Americas
Jennifer Anne Moses — Visiting Hours

Fomite

Charles Opara — How Hamisu Survived Bad Kidneys
and a Bad Son-in-Law
Martin Ott — Interrogations
George Ovitt — The Showcase
Christopher Peterson — Amoebic Simulacra
Christopher Peterson — Scratch the Itchy Teeth
Charles Phillips — Dead South
Jack Pulaski — Love's Labours
Charles Rafferty — Saturday Night at Magellan's
Joseph Rathgeber — Bad Days on the Batso
Mohsen Rezaei — The Violet Needle
Ron Savage — What We Do For Love
Vince Sgambati — Undertow of Memory
Fred Skolnik— Americans and Other Stories
Lynn Sloan — This Far Is Not Far Enough
L.E. Smith — Views Cost Extra
Caitlin Hamilton Summie — To Lay To Rest Our Ghosts
Susan Thomas — Among Angelic Orders
Tom Walker — Signed Confessions
Silas Dent Zobal — The Inconvenience of the Wings

For more information or to order any of our books, visit:
fomitepress.com/our-books.html

www.ingramcontent.com/pod-product-compliance
Lightning Source LLC
Chambersburg PA
CBHW070506200726

48293CB00007B/2417